Factor 2025

Johnny Tait

www.johnnytait.com

Johnny Tait is a successful stand-up comedian, often billed as "The Cockney Comic" he has performed all over the world in a variety of venues, from the most luxurious of theatres to the roughest and the toughest of clubs.

He has made a few appearances on television and has worked alongside some of the biggest names in show-business.

His first novel 'Conscience' was adapted to a stage play that has toured all over the U.K.

"When I said I was going to be a comedian, everybody laughed. They're not laughing now."

The comedy genius Bob Monkhouse

Why did I write 'Factor 2025?'

My entertainment career begun in 1977.
Since then I have experienced all the ups and downs of show business and feel that television does not portray variety as it is.
I would say if your knowledge of the entertainment industry is based on what you have seen on television you know nothing. In fact I would be bold enough to say that if your knowledge of show business is based solely on what you have seen on television you know less than nothing.
We see on television talent shows participants telling the audience things like "I was bullied at school and it was my singing that got me through."
The reality is that when you are performing the audience do not wish to know about your personal problems and do not care whether or not you were bullied at school.
We see on television talent shows contestants crying for all manner of reasons, sometimes because they are happy

with the comments the judges have made, other times because the judges have rejected them.

In the real world if you display any sign of weakness in some of the clubs we perform in the audience will eat you alive.

I'm sure everyone is now aware that what is shown on television as the first audition, is in fact the second or third.

The producers know what the participants can and cannot do and they have researched their backgrounds before they are presented to us on the telly.

Is it morally correct to take a person or person's that think they can sing or dance or have some kind of talent that could set them onto a career in show business, then present them on national television just to publicly humiliate them?

Are the show producers concerned about the damage they may be doing to an individual's self-esteem?

Are viewing figures such an important factor that morals don't even come into it?

When I was a teenage lad in the seventies becoming a Butlins Redcoat was seen as the first step towards a career in showbiz. That is how it all started for me, and within my first week I was performing in The Gaiety Theatre in a packed house performing to an audience of 1,652.

Nobody said it would be easy. We would rehearse some nights till 2 a.m.

In those days there was no such thing as set hours, the saying was "You said you could do it when you wrote in."

Our working hours were non applicable and the normal working week would be about 90 hours.

But nobody ever complained it was the job we loved and at the time there was nothing else that I would rather do.

Despite the fact that being a Redcoat was the first stepping stone, only about 1% of Redcoats go on to make a lifelong career in the rollercoaster world of showbiz.

Certainly anyone that publicly snivels like they do on T.V talent shows when they are upset would never make it.

In the year 2001 I was appearing on an important showcase at Stratford-Upon-Avon.

At the time it was the biggest showcase in mainstream variety.

My youngest brother unaware of this called me two hours before I was due to go on stage to inform me that our sister Jackie had just a couple of days left to live.

I absolutely worship Jackie.

You may think, well he's bound to say nice things about his sister, people always say nice things about their loved ones when they have passed away. However they really feel about them.

The case here is: My sister Jackie was the nicest person anybody could ever wish to meet. I absolutely adored her.

Jackie was the backbone of our family.

She had married her first boyfriend and went on to have two beautiful children Johnny and Leanne.

Now in her early forties Jackie was on her death bed.

I cannot describe the way I was feeling, my Mother was also terminally ill and was housebound. I just wanted to rush back to London to be with my family.

But before that I performed in a packed civic centre before an audience consisting of agents and bookers.

They did not know about my grief then. I never told them. 99.9% of them still do not know.

You see the thing is nobody wants to know about your personal anguish.

Can you deliver the goods?

That is all anybody is interested in.

So why do people that participate in television talent shows stand there and snivel?

I have been fortunate enough to have made a career as a stand-up comedian. In the real world in order to be able to do that it is important to be able to adjust to any audience in any type of venue. I have the pleasure of performing in some of the world's most beautiful venues, I have also worked in venues in which, if the audience let the entertainer live, that would be considered a good gig.

The highlight of my career was being asked by showbiz legend Joe Longthorne, after he had seen me perform in a charity show in Blackpool "Would you like to be my support act on my forthcoming tour?" I did not need to be asked twice and needed no prompting whatsoever, I jumped at the opportunity.

Throughout my career I have had some amazing standing ovations, I have also died a few deaths in which the ground could not have swallowed me up soon enough.
The thing is television does not portray showbiz the way it really is, television talent shows could not possibly be any further away from the reality of what light entertainment really is about.
They make entertainers look weak and pathetic, when the reality is if you want to make a career in showbiz, you need to have skin as thick as the rear end of a Rhinocerous.

Factor 2025 is a fictional tale of how I foresee the future of television talent shows.
I would like to add that any resemblance to any persons or person living or dead is purely coincidental.
Because I cannot afford to be sued.

"Entertainment is about as glamorous as changing the sheets in a bedwetting clinic"

Les Dawson

Done What?

'They have done what?' Powell bawled into the telephone.
'And whose decision was that………….?'
'The board, the board, you are telling me the board have
decided to take my show away from prime time TV and
put it on channel five ………. On a Thursday afternoon!
You have got to be joking. You have got to be joking!
Get them on the phone, I want to speak to them now ……
Well get them and call me when you have.'
The moment he had feared had finally arrived.
Due to the viewing figures of the last series dropping to an
all-time low, the board of control had decided they could
not give him the most valuable air time any longer,
regardless of how much he offered to pay for it.
He started pacing the floor 'Why did I not see this coming
sooner? I knew this would happen one day. Why did I not
do something about it before it came to this?'

These were the questions he was asking himself.

After the last series had flopped so badly, the television company sent their own researchers out onto the streets to speak with the viewing public.

The board then arranged a subsequent meeting with Powell to tell him about their findings and ask him to explain how he was going to react to them.

The findings from the questionnaire were:

22% of the people questioned said they watched the show and would carry-on watching.

32% stated that they did not watch a great deal of television and had no intention of ever watching a talent show.

46% of the people surveyed answered that they had stopped watching The Factor and did not intend on ever watching it again.

It was the 46% that had stopped tuning into The Factor that the board were most interested in.

They were offered a small reward in the shape of a bar of chocolate if they were kind enough to take part in a short survey.

The findings from the survey were read out to Powell, along with some of the comments made by the people that had taken part.

"It's got far too boring it's the same type of thing over and over again"

"The two blokes on the side of the stage just get on my nerves, why are they there? They are not funny and what they say doesn't make any sense either."

"I got fed up with moaners snivelling and whining about how they got bullied at school. Everybody has been bullied at one time or another, but we don't spend our lives moaning about it"

"It's obviously a fix anybody with any degree of intelligence can see"

"Trenton Powell gets on my tits, he is such a self-righteous big-head"

The large gentlemen that sat directly opposite Powell on the other side of the table, wearing a dark grey suit with a navy blue tie removed his glasses after he had read the quotations and stated 'These comments are the most common amongst those made by the viewers and we feel that unless they are addressed and a solution found, we may have to remove The Factor from its allocated slot.' To which the other four board members just nodded in agreement whilst giving Powell a stony faced look.
Powell felt the anger raging inside of him. He was as egotistical as anybody could possibly be, how dare anybody criticise him in this manner?
When he replied he did so in a remarkably controlled way. 'I accept that my own researchers have failed to spot the reasons for the fall in viewing figures and I thank you for

bringing your findings to my attention and I intend to personally resolve these matters immediately in order to put The Factor back on top of the ratings.'

He left the meeting feeling like a naughty schoolboy that had just been chastised by his headmaster, he was angry very angry.

He was mumbling to himself 'How dare that bunch of schmucks talk to me in that manner? How dare they even think about moving my show from the prime slot? I could buy and sell the lot of them. The television company would be nothing without me.'

Despite his anger Powell knew that he would have to make significant changes in order to appease the board, so he set about his clean-up operation.

He decided the first move would be to get rid of the dead wood, the cretins that contributed nothing to the show and brought about the criticism and the drop in viewing figures.

Sacking Tone and Daz (The two blokes on the side of the stage) was not an easy task, as like himself, they had also came from a privileged background.

They had also contributed to the funding of the show from the very beginning, so therefore when he informed them that "It was felt that they should leave the show and work on a project of their own, and he would gift them with £200,000 as a matter of goodwill" They protested loudly and threatened to sue the arse off Powell.

But the advice from Tone's father who just so happened to be a solicitor was too "Take the sum offered to them and walk away, as a lawsuit would be costly and could drag on

forever. And the adverse publicity it could generate would be damaging to their personal careers in the long term."
So thanks to Tones father that boil on Powell's bum had been lanced.

There was no love lost between them as Powell's personal opinion of Daz and Tone was that they were totally irritating and completely void of any talent whatsoever.
The only reason they were on-board was due to their financial input. Now that they had ceased to be of any use, it was good riddance.

Whilst their opinion of Powell was that he was an arrogant egotistical old fart, and if he went any further up his own arsehole he would disappear altogether.

Daz and Tone had also lost interest in The Factor, they were only interested in their own personal fame.

So there was no leaving party, no hugging or hearty handshakes, just a £200,000 settlement and a termination of their contracts.

Sacking his researchers was a much easier task, there was no pay-off, no explanations or objections. He just simply sent them an e-mail stating "The standard of your work is wholly unsatisfactory therefore your employment with Power-Man Productions is terminated forthwith"

Not only did this not cause Powell any hardship, it actually gave him a sense of smug satisfaction.

Sacking the members of Power-Man team that he held responsible for the dramatic fall in the viewing figures did not satisfy the board.

They did not see that as a solution to the problem.

As far as they were concerned he had not presented them with a suitable resolve as they had requested.

And so the day that his own arrogance had prevented him from seeing coming, had finally arrived.

The bomb shell had been dropped, the show was to be moved from television's top slot.

No more would he be "Mister Show-Biz himself." The name he called himself as he admired his own appearance whenever he looked into a mirror, like Narcissus every time he saw his own reflection.

Monday Morning

It was a wet Monday morning, the rain was drizzling.
As Powell stepped from his chauffeur driven limousine, he glanced at his gold Rolex watch, the time was eleven forty five.
He didn't normally do Monday mornings, in fact he rarely got up before midday these days, but the show needed a severe kick up the backside, so Powell had got up at six thirty that morning in order to make his way to the airport.
As he was travelling to the studio he was cursing his employees for their incompetence, vowing to himself that before the end of the day he would sack at least one of the remaining members of the team in the most humiliating way that he could possibly think of.
Powell didn't have any hobbies in the way that most people think of hobbies, his favourite pastime was making money and to boost his already inflated ego he liked to be seen in public with glamorous women half his age.
Now well into his late fifties and despite a small fortune spent on cosmetic surgery and the strict health regimes he would occasionally put himself on, the years of over indulgence had taken their toll, the wrinkles had started to show and the middle aged spread, along with man-boobs had appeared.
Powell was definitely no Adonis.

So the 6ft glamorous models that he regularly had on his arm did not impress anybody.

"She's obviously only with him for his money"

"I wonder how much she charges him to be his escort"

"She's only with him for his wallet"

Were among the comments people made.

Of course nobody ever dared say this to his face, as he had the fieriest of tempers and an extremely vengeful nature. Anybody that crossed him in the slightest way felt the full force of his wrath.

Waiting for Powell in the studio was Mellissa, an extremely attractive young lady, at just twenty eight years of age, was the very definition of beauty. Six feet tall with legs that went right up to her bum and a slim but curvaceous figure.

Mellissa had landed her first modelling contract at the age of eighteen, but did not become a household name until the day of her twenty first birthday when she entered the household of a reality television show, in which a dozen people that had never met each other before were locked inside the house and were not permitted to communicate in anyway with anyone outside.

Neither could they watch T.V or listen to the radio.

World war three could have broken out and they would have been none the wiser.

But there were microphones all over the household broadcasting every sound they made and every word they spoke. Cameras were in every room, everything tiny little thing the housemates did was there for anyone tuning into We're Watching to see and hear.

The only room exempt from sound and vision to the whole nation was the lavatory, even now that voyeurism had become acceptable by a proportion of the population as a form of entertainment, nobody wanted to see or be seen by anybody else defecating.

In the day and age where some members of society have lost all sense of dignity, pride and self-respect, it is nice to know that some things have remained sacred.

So the housemates viewed the lavatory as hallowed turf. Channel We're Watching was broadcasting their every movement 24 hours a day.

So therefore the lavatory was the one place they could safely go without the eyes and ears of another soul watching over them.

Of course they spent more time in the lavatory than a person normally would, because it was the only place in the entire household that they could masturbate without a camera picking them up and broadcasting their moment of self-gratification to the whole nation.

The only rule regarding the smallest room in the threshold was that:

"Housemates are only permitted to enter the room alone." The producers wanted any form of physical contact made between housemates to be broadcast.

Their theory being that twelve young people would not be able to live together in close proximity without personal relationships developing, which is exactly what they wanted as that what was they saw as the key to boosting viewing figures.

Mellissa much to the disappointment of the producers, never showed any sign of sexual attraction towards any of her housemates. Her kind mild mannered good nature, frustrated the producers, because that was not what the voyeurs (Sorry Viewers) were tuning in for.

Nobody was interested in a good girl.

Then one evening when the housemates were supplied with large amounts of alcohol and instructed to play a game called "Truth or Dare" Mellissa shocked everyone including herself, when she accepted the dare that had been put to her, by stripping naked and dancing on the lounge coffee table whilst singing at the top of her voice "I'm just a girl who can't say no."

Her popularity soared, viewing figures doubled.

The national tabloid newspaper (I use the term newspaper very loosely) that boasted to be:

"The official newspaper of We're Watching" plastered her pics all over the paper including the front page.

The producers were delighted. Mellissa, much to the dismay of the housemates that dared her to do something they thought she would not dare do, was voted the winner by the viewing public, giving her a £50,000 payday, which also led to her being offered further modelling contracts for lads magazines, and for a while Mellissa was a regular feature in the tabloid papers and the gossip mags.

Now here she was employed by Powell as a judge/critic on his reality television talent show.

When most people enter the workplace they begin by wishing their colleagues a "Good morning"

Or maybe they ask "How was your weekend?"

Not Powell when he entered the studio he launched straight into his favourite subject, himself 'Do you know when I was a kid my father passed away from war injuries he received when he was fighting to defend our country whilst on active service, leaving my grieving mother with five young children to bring up on her own?'

Mellissa had heard this tale many times before and it always made her feel uncomfortable as she did not know how to respond, she just nodded her head politely.

Powell carried on 'Oh! Yes I was brought up without a father, my father lost his life when I was a young lad, so the people of Great Britain would be free, but I did not want my brothers and sisters to go without, so I did not one but two paper rounds, so that I could buy birthday presents and Christmas presents for my younger brothers and sisters. You see when I was a kid if a person wanted something they had to work for it. There was no such thing as a free lunch no. If you wanted it you worked for it. Then I left school at the age of sixteen with no G.C.E's or 'O' levels or any of that nonsense whatsoever and so I started working on the street markets as a general dogsbody for the traders. All day long it was "Carry that" "Fetch me this" For just a few pounds a week I was at their beck and call. Then I realised I had more brains than all of them schmucks that I was schlepping for had put together.

So I got my own market stall, I grafted seven days a week and within a year I had seven market stalls, people were now working for me. Then I decided to go into the music industry, I had my own recording studios, with my own record label and by the time I was twenty five years old, I was a millionaire. Oh! Yes I went from leaving school at the age of sixteen without a pot to piss in to becoming a millionaire within the space of nine years.'

He stopped speaking and just stood there looking at Mellissa.

She did not like this, the silence made her feel uncomfortable, she then took it that his silence was a cue for her to respond, when she spoke Mellissa spoke softly in an approving way.

'It's remarkable, people have so much admiration for you, and they love your rags to riches story.'

Powell smirked it was his usual self-appreciating smirk, you know the smirk he gives that makes you want to smack him around the face with a wet packet of shit.

He loved to receive a compliment and everyone that worked for him knew that that was the way to stay employed.

With a shrug of his shoulders he replied.

'Of course they do, it's a great story, but what they don't know is, it's just a load of bullshit. I never had any market stalls or record companies and I certainly didn't need to do any paper round to earn spending money. I was an only child, I never really knew my parents they were always busy "Socialites" was what they called themselves and they were filthy rich. I was brought up by a nanny or an "au pair" as they say in Sweden. I never experienced a mother's love. Then when I was ten years old my parents sent me away to a boarding school. It was full of poor little rich kids that nobody wanted. I hardly ever saw my parents, except on the occasional event for families, then I was dressed up and put on display like a trophy or a piece of jewellery. Despite the way my parents neglected me I was never short of money. For my eighteenth birthday my father bought me a beautiful gleaming red Ferrari. How I loved that car it was a right fanny magnet. Could I pull the crumpet in that?' Powell paused.

Mellissa was hoping he did not want a reply to the question. She strongly disliked women being referred to as "Crumpet" She also knew that it would be a big mistake to challenge him. So she just nodded her head slowly then picked up the tumbler glass in front of her and took a sip of water.

Thankfully he carried on without waiting for her response. 'The problem was I had this right posh voice, I spoke like I had a dozen plums in my mouth, it was all "O.K Yah" "Jolly Spiffing" "Super" That was definitely not the image I wanted to portray. I wanted to be seen as a man of the people, for the people. So do you know what I did? I got this Cockney barrow boy and I offered him ten thousand pounds to teach me to speak with a working class accent, and do you know what he said? He said "For ten grand I'll teach you to talk anyway you like governor." So I was with him for every waking hour for four weeks. I remember the first day, he said:

"We'll start with an easy one, repeat after me. "Free undred and firty free fousand feavers on a frushes froat sum are fickuns and sum are finnuns."

Then he got me saying:

"Put on the Dickie Dirt, the Daisy Locks, the Whistle and Flute, the Ones and Twos and the Peckham Rye, go down the Apples and Pears, up the Frog and Toad around the Jack Horner in the Rub-a Dub for a Pig's Ear pay with my Nelson Eddie's and clock the Bar Maid with the huge Bristol Cities and the gorgeous Bottle and Glass."

Now that I had lost my phoney public school boy accent, and had the image I wanted I produced The Factor.

For years it was the most popular show on television, with more viewers than any other show in the history of T.V. It absolutely kicked the shit out of live entertainment. Theatre attendances dropped to an all-time low, the pubs and the social clubs all over the country really suffered, every Saturday night the public were at home glued to the box, and I became a household name.'

As he said "Household name" Powell held his arms outstretched up to his side with his palms open in a manner of self-appreciation, or as a performer taking an accolade from the audience for putting on an exceptional performance.

Mellissa saw this as an opportunity to flatter the boss, she stood up and with a smile remarked 'You were in the papers every day, television camera's followed you everywhere you went. Everyman wants to be you, and every woman wants to be with you.'

Powell just looked at her and smirked

'Yeh and you know it.'

He stood there for a few a moments nodding his head in praise of himself, then suddenly his mood changed and his tone became aggressive.

He leant on the table with his right hand palm and staring Mellissa straight in the eyes he barked.

'And now look what's happened, the viewing figures are down by seventy three percent, advertising revenue down by sixty eight percent and on the last series we had less than a third of the phone in voters than we had previously. And now they have taken us from the prime time Saturday night spot, to Thursday afternoon! And if that is not bad enough they have moved us to channel five. Channel fucking five. Channel five is not for A list celebrity's like me, it's for burnt out old has beens like Noel Edmonds. What the hell are they thinking about? What is going on?

As he asked the question he threw his arms in the air then turned his back on Mellissa, he was looking around the studio, as if he was waiting for a magical fairy to appear and answer his questions.

Mellissa was now feeling very uneasy as she looked at the back of his well-groomed hair and his grey flannel trousers, which he had pulled up above his waist higher than necessary over his navy blue V neck jumper. She wondered whether she should reply to his question or not.

She did not need to guess any longer Powell turned, looked her in the eye and without saying a word gestured for her to answer.

She had seen that look in his eye before, it made her nervous she answered in a soft quiet tone.

'It might be because the people think the voting is rigged.'

'The voting is not rigged.'

Powell replied with an angry tone, then pointing his finger at Mellissa he raised his voice as he repeated. 'The voting is not rigged, don't you dare say the voting is rigged.'

Defensively she replied 'I know the voting is not rigged, but it was the newspaper's they hinted at it, and I think some of the people believed it.'

Powell was now pacing around the large sparsely furnished space, whilst he did so he shook his head as he spoke 'It wasn't in all the newspapers, it was just the one and what they know about it anyway? What does anyone know about it? And as for the public, we'll they will believe anything they see in print. That aside, all publicity is good publicity, if you say something's bad people will watch it. There's only one thing worse than bad publicity, and do you know what that is? Well do yer?'

Mellissa replied timidly 'No I'm sorry I don't.'

'No publicity.' Powell barked. 'The only thing worse than bad publicity is no publicity and that's the problem, we aren't getting the publicity we use to get, we were on the front page of all the tabloid's we filled practically every page of the gossip mags.'

Just then a young assistant entered the studio, she didn't knock, everybody knocks, nobody just walks into a room that Trenton Powell is in without knocking, but Nicola did and she was right on cue as if she had been waiting in the wings like an actor listening for her cue line to take to the stage 'I have looked through them.' She stated.

This infuriated Powell, among the many things that he hated being interrupted was one of them. 'Looked through them, looked through them, what the hell you are talking about?'

The realisation that one has just angered the boss would normally send any employee of Power-Man Productions into a mad panic.

But not Nicola at just nineteen years of age and weighing a little under nine stone, the youngest and smallest member of the team was in no way intimidated by Powell. She replied with an air of self-confidence. 'This month's magazines and today's newspapers, you asked me to look, to see if we are in them.'

'So where are they? Let's see them.' Powell demanded. Nicola had no magazines or newspapers on her person, her hands were bare, it was obvious that anybody could see that, but all the same she held out her hands and showed her empty palms as she stated. 'There is nothing we didn't make the press this month.'

For a man that craved power and fame and strongly believed that his show was the most significant thing happening in today's society to go a whole month without any media exposure was totally unacceptable and completely unbelievable.

'Didn't make the press. Didn't make the press. You have got to be joking, you have got to be fucking joking. Are you trying to tell me that the whole entire show and every single person that is connected with it did not get a single snap shot or the slightest mention in any of the gossip mags this month? Are you saying that we have not had one tiny little article in the tabloid press?'

'I'm afraid so Mister Powell, I went through them all and there is nothing.'

Looking away from the young girl whose name he did not know and did not care to know, the only thing Powell knew about her, and cared about, was that she was on a work experience scheme so he did not need to pay her. He turned to Mellissa and asked. 'Mellissa why do you think I have got you on my show?'

'Because I have got an extensive knowledge of ……….'

Powell did not allow her to finish her reply. He cut in with an aggressive tone. 'Because you have got what the gossip papers want, and yet you have not made a single feature for the past five weeks.'

'Six weeks.' Nicola informed him.

'Six weeks six bloody weeks.' Powell barked at the top of his voice. 'Mellissa what the bloody hell are doing?'

Even though young Nicola did not fear the boss, she now felt her pale white face surrounded by a mane of thick black wavy hair instantly turning into a deep shade of red. Because she now felt responsible for the anger that was being vented at Mellissa, not knowing how to deal with the situation she now found herself in she turned on her heels and exited the room, whilst Powell's yelling echoed all around and pounded through her ears.

'You should be out there, drumming up the publicity, not sitting at home watching television. We make television. We are television.'

This was a side to Powell's character that Mellissa did not like to see. There were occasions when he could be quite charming towards her. Whenever he had taken her out for a social evening he had said the sweetest things, paid her an abundance of compliments and made her feel like a princess. But now, at this moment, she felt like a defenceless rabbit trapped in the jaws of a fox.

She tried to pacify him. 'But I'm doing everything I can, when I was on holiday last week in Gran Canaria I went topless on the beach all the time, the only thing I wore was a tiny thong, then in the evenings when we went to the restaurants and clubs, I was wearing see through top's and I never once wore a bra.'

Looking around the room in a totally ridiculous way as if he did not know his whereabouts, in order to emphasis his point, Powel asked. 'So where are they? Where are the snaps? More to the point, where were they? Where were the paparazzi? Why were they not informed?'

'My boyfriend called them and told them where we would be.'

'Your boyfriend, your boyfriend. You're telling me you left it to your boyfriend, so come on tell me about your boyfriend?'

'His name is Joseph and he works with computers.'

A twinkle appeared in Mellissa's eye and a smile spread across her face whenever she mentioned Joseph's name.

A disdainful grin spread across Powell's face as he stood there slowly clapping his hands together. He was not applauding like an appreciative audience, he was mocking as he sarcastically said. 'That is brilliant that is a work of genius, I put millions of pounds into my show and you go on holiday with Joseph who works with computers. It's no wonder you've not made the pages, who wants to know about Joseph who works with computers?'

'But he's really sweet, everybody likes him and we're planning to get married next year.'

'No, no that is not good enough we have got to get you a man that will grab the media attention. I've got it there's a footballer, he came over here from Somalia seven years ago. At the age of eleven he was recruited into the rebel army as a boy soldier, then when he was eighteen he was spotted kicking a football about by a talent scout and was taken out of the war zone and brought to England. Now at the ripe young age of twenty five the press are all over him. He has just signed a three year contract with a top premiership club, but at the moment he is on a five match ban for head-butting another player. And the best part is, last week the police stopped him for speeding in his B.M.W, they then found two ounces of wacky-backy and a bag of cocaine in his car, he was arrested and to add to it as well as dangerous driving and possession of drugs, he has also been charged with assaulting a police officer. The press are absolutely loving him. He has been headline news in all of the tabloid papers for the past few weeks. What we need to do is get him on-board. Now what I will do is arrange with his agent for the two of you to go off together for a couple of days, somewhere warm and exotic. A romantic beach holiday in Saint Tropez, you get your tit's out and I will inform the paparazzi, they will love it. Everyone will love it.'

Standing there in pure admiration of himself for thinking up such a genius way to save the show and bring back the viewer's Powell did not see the tears welling up in Mellissa's eyes. Not that he would have cared anyway. Choking back the tears she replied. 'I can't do that.'

'You will do that.'

'But what about my boyfriend Joseph?'

'This is not about you boyfriend Joseph. This is about the show. My show. And nobody, but nobody is bigger than my show. The world is a stage and each must play his part, or in your case, her part. Can you just think about this for one second? How many women would love your job? How many women would love me for a boss? How many women would love a boss that pays for them to jet off to the sun? You just don't know how lucky you are, do you?' Powell was looking at Mellissa and shaking his head slowly from side to side as she pleaded.

'But please Mister Powell don't make me do that. Joseph would be so upset and I'm afraid that it could ruin our relationship. Please don't make me do it. I have been thinking of a way of getting the viewing figures up and I have got an idea if we …..'

Again she was not given the opportunity to finish her statement.

'You've been thinking! You've got an idea! You need brains to think and have an idea. Stand up, come on now stand up, now put your hands on the table like that' Powell leant forward as he spoke he put his open palms flat on the five feet long wooden table with his feet twelve inches apart. Mellissa done as she was told, she mimicked his stance. Powell then stood approximately four feet behind her and holding up a mirror he said. 'Now look over your shoulder and tell me what you see.'

'A mirror.'

The reply she received to that answer was spoken as sarcastically as it could possibly have been. 'Very clever a mirror, my my, you have got brains. Now tell me, what can you see in the mirror?'

'My bum.'

'Absolutely spot on your bum, and that is why you are here. When I first met you, about eighteen months ago I noticed that you had the cutest little bum I have ever seen.' As he spoke Powell stepped forward and cupping his left hand he squeezed the poor girl's buttocks, not affectionately or playfully, but to demonstrate that he was in control of the situation and could grope her anyway and anywhere he pleased. Then turning to lean the mirror against the wall behind him he barked. 'So don't tell me what you think, I am not interested in what you think, I am only interested in your cute little arse, I am not interested in what you think.'

Mellissa sat herself back down onto the wooden chair and as she was struggling to fight back the tears she pleaded. 'I'm sorry Mister Powell, but please don't make me go on holiday with that footballer.'

Powell softened his voice and smiled as he replied. 'It's alright you don't have to go if you don't want to, nobody has to do anything they don't want to.'

'Thank you Mister Powell, thank you so much.'

'Now get your cute little bum out of my sight, there's thousands more where you came from, I can replace you as easy as that.'

As he finished the sentence Powell clicked his fingers to emphasis the "Easy as that."

Mellissa was not holding back the tears any longer, the humiliation she felt from being forced to stand with her legs apart whilst her buttocks were groped in an abusive manner coupled with losing her job, sent the tears flooding down her face 'But I don't want to go, I love working for you sir, please don't fire me, I'll do anything you ask.'

As the tears were streaming down the young lady's face, a sadistic self-satisfying smirk appeared on the face of the middle aged bully, as he spoke he nodded his head slowly encouraging Mellissa to mirror his actions. She did so like a Lemming following another over a cliff.

'A weekend in Saint Tropez?' They both slowly nodded 'With a Somalian footballer?' Again they both nodded, Powell smirked as she struggled to fight back the tears. 'Maybe even snort a bit of coke, and forget about Joseph who works with computers.'

Feeling pleased that he could manipulate her to do anything he wanted her to do even though it was totally against her will, and feeling satisfied that he found a solution to win back media attention and improve the shows fallen ratings, Powell sat next to Mellissa, gave her hand a gentle squeeze as he smiled. 'Right now let's get on with it, let's do what we do, what have you got for me?'

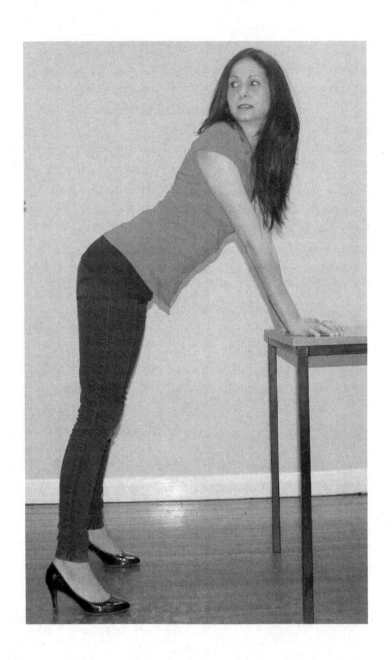

The Green Room

Along the grey dull corridor just twenty yards from the studio was the green room.

The term green room brings to mind a cosy hospitality suite decorated with an abundance of soft furniture, small wooden coffee tables, a microwave on a makeshift kitchen surface in the corner a few feet away from the stainless steel sink, and an assortment of soft drinks and snacks for the artistes to help themselves too whilst they are waiting to perform.

Now this particular green room was nothing like that.

It was a large hall with off white painted brickwork, there was hardly any furniture, just a few uncomfortable plastic chairs. Certainly not enough to accommodate the eight hundred plus hopefuls that had crammed inside. Some of which had the foresight to bring their own picnic chairs, those that did not have a chair sat on the cold concrete floor or just stood and leant against the wall.

They could help themselves to as many soft drinks and snacks as they wanted by purchasing them from one of the vending machines that had been strategically placed around the hall for their convenience.

"Two pounds fifty for a bottle of water and two pound eighty for a packet of crisps, and the bloody machine didn't even give me any change. It's a rip off, that's what it is, a bloody rip off."

Complained a forty something year old man at the top of his voice. Not to anybody in particular but to anybody that cared to listen to his rant. Before he went back to the empty spot he had reserved for himself by placing an old grey coat neatly folded against the wall.

There was a camera crew operating in the hall, at that moment they were filming a short chubby man dressed as what one would describe as a pantomime dame.

When he was asked what he thought he would bring to the show, the reply he gave was.

"Talent and glamour darling. Two qualities that I have in total abundance."

He then proceeded to sing as loudly and as high as he possibly could in a key that nobody has ever heard before, because it has not yet been invented and is never likely to ever be. "The hills are alive with the sound of music." Everybody in the hall knew that this man would be a certainty to pass the initial audition and be sent through to the televised stages of The Factor.

Despite the fact that each and every-one of the candidates were hoping that today's audition would launch a career for them in the world of show business, deep in their hearts they all knew that The Factor was nothing more than a freak show that was set up to massage the producers

already inflated ego and enlarge his bank account.
Surprisingly less than half of them understood that they
were just cannon fodder for the smug faced barstard's that
looked down their noses at them, whilst giving their
verdict in a condescending manner, like magistrates
sentencing some poor innocent soul that they had just
found guilty.

In one corner of the room was a man dressed as a
Neanderthal, wearing a leopard skin leotard and sporting
long hair way past his shoulders that did not look like it
had been washed or brushed for months and a long
unkempt beard.

He was attempting to juggle four brightly coloured balls,
red, blue, yellow and green whilst balancing on a unicycle.
Much to the amusement of everyone in the vicinity as he
kept falling off.

This attracted the attention of the camera crew that
requested. "Can you try that just one more time?" each
time the hapless caveman hit the deck. The crew wanted to
be sure that one was in the can. An absolute certainty to be
given air-time.

Next up the crew were informed of a newly engaged
couple that were hoping to announce their marriage plans
on national television to Powell and the viewing nation.
They were dressed as Batman and Wonder Woman.
Have you ever heard the saying "Opposites attract?"
This newly betrothed couple really did appear to be a
complete mismatch. Apart from the fact that they both had
a fetish for dressing up as comic book super heroes and

they both had a desire to make complete and utter fools of themselves on national television.

They really did appear to have nothing in common.

Batman was twenty years old, six foot five inches tall and painfully thin. Whilst Wonder-woman was fifty seven years of age, five foot four inches tall with the physique of a Russian shot-putter. When she was asked her weight, she politely replied. "That's none of your fucking business." The crew instantly knew that they were definitely right for the show, a relationship with a wide age difference and a physical mismatch, coupled with a foul mouth.

This must be compulsive viewing. They were about as suitably matched as Adolf Hitler and Martin Luther King. Which made them a dead certainty to be on the show. Everyone knew there was no need for a debate.

Anyone that knew anything about The Factor knew that they were exactly what the producer was looking for, there was no way Powell would ever turn them away.

On the other side of the hall was another tall thin young man dressed in a superman costume, he was eating an endless amount of baked beans as fast as he possibly could whilst stopping at times to lean forward and ignite one of his farts. This drew mixed feelings from the people around him, some found it amusing whilst others looked on in disgust.

When the crew spoke with him he said his hobbies were. "Playing video games and watching pornographic films." No need to say another word, he qualified for the show. These were just a few of the total eccentrics that were sure to get their ten minutes of fame.

But the majority of people that had been informed to register for the audition at the front desk at 9 a.m. were just ordinary everyday people hoping to escapes their dull humdrum lives and live the dream.

Consequently the majority of the keen hopefuls had arrived early, by 7.30 a.m. there was at least seven hundred of them queuing along the pavement, in the pouring rain waiting for the doors to open.

The rain ceased for approximately fifteen minutes, that was when the camera crew ceased the opportunity to film the masses in the queue, they were instructing the people when to smile and cheer.

At one stage a man with a loud hailer informed the queue of hopefuls that a black stretch limousine would shortly be passing and on the word "Now" they were to applaud and cheer as loudly and enthusiastically as they possibly could whilst smiling and focusing their gaze on the limousine. Of course there was nobody in the car, but when the programme was edited Trenton Powell would be seen getting out of the vehicle and stepping onto a red carpet that had barriers on each side to keep back the photographers and autograph hunters.

For the hopefuls today was their day. Today was the day of their audition for a chance to appear on The Factor and they had been informed that they would be performing for the main man himself, something that had never happened before at this stage of the auditions.

It was a long day for the hopefuls, with some of them having travelled through the night in order to be there on time.

Every-one of them on entering the building was given a number, written on a piece of sticky back paper, which they were told to place on their chest, then they were ushered into the green room.

The large clock on one of the bare walls showed the time. It was now two minutes to twelve and not a single person had yet been called through to the studio to be auditioned. Then suddenly a voice came over the public address system: "Number four thousand seven hundred and eighty two. Mister Powell will see you now."

Everybody immediately looked down at the number that they had stuck on their chests as the first of today's auditionee's followed the floorwalker through the green double doors.

Amellia

Whilst reading from the notes that were attached to the clipboard in front of her Mellissa Stated 'We have a girl that I have seen personally, and I spoke with her for quite a long time. Her name is Amellia she is eighteen years old and she lives at home with her parents and her two younger brothers. Amellia is still at school studying for her 'A' levels she says "I want to work with elderly people as I love speaking with them, and I find the tales they tell about their experiences in life so interesting." But this is the bit that I really like, she also says "I do not want to sing professionally but I would like to be able to do it part time in order to earn extra money to support charities like help the aged."

'Will you not waste my time?' Replied Powell as he pointed to his gold wristwatch. 'Nobody is interested in an eighteen year old girl that lives with her parents and wants to sing part time.'

Mellissa knew she had to tread carefully. Powell hated anybody questioning his judgement and the one thing she did not want to do was make him angry, this would be her second series working on The Factor and she knew that any day could be her last, as he would not hesitate to dismiss her in the same manner that he terminated the employment of the other girls that occupied the part that she now played, if she failed to please him. Although

Mellissa felt that she could secure her position within Power-man productions by making a positive contribution, so she bravely carried on 'But she's an amazing singer, she writes all of her own songs, and I think her interest in old people would make a good angle.'

Powell replied through gritted teeth. 'I don't care what she sings like and I don't care if she writes her own songs, and who gives two hoots about elderly people? What we need is characters, not sweet sickly nice characters, we need characters with a bit of oomph in them you know the type the public want to see.'

Mellissa knew that she was treading on thin ice, the wise thing would have been to instruct the floorwalkers to send Amellia home, but she really felt that she could impress the boss with her creative input, so she put her hands together as if she was praying and added 'Amellia really is unique, she is attractive in her own individual way and her voice really sets her aside from any of the others that I have heard, and I am sure that when you hear her you will put her on the show………… Please.

'Alright she's got two minutes.'

Mellissa picked up the handset that was placed on the table in front of her, pushed a button and called for 'Amellia Number four thousand seven hundred and eighty two.'

If any member of Powell's team ever dared to advise him that he should put somebody on the show, the way to assert his authority was to do the exact opposite and reject them. He sat there with his arms folded across his chest, his mind was set, there was no way Amellia would be appearing on The Factor. Poor Amellia was flocking a dead horse.

The door opened and Amellia entered with a spring in her step and a twinkle in her eye, she smiled sweetly but did not speak until Mellissa acknowledged her as she spoke 'Hello Amellia, it's good to see you again, tell Mister Powell a little bit about yourself.'

'My name's Amellia.'

'Look into the camera for me Darling.' Called out Jason the camp camera man, who called everyone "Darling" because he felt that was what a luvvie should do.

Amellia looked into the camera and repeated 'My name's Amellia.'

Doing his best to look as uninterested as he possibly could Powell remarked 'I know that, I've heard it said a thousand times already.'

Amellia did not react to his comment, she just carried on speaking 'I first starting singing at Sunday school when I was five years old, then I joined the church choir. I like singing with them very much. I also like to help my mother with the chores around the house as she is disabled. And in my spare time I am a volunteer in a care home for the elderly. I love older people.'

Doing his best to sound as sarcastic as he possibly could, Powell retorted 'That is interesting the viewers will be glued to their television sets. Go on then sing.'

Without speaking another word Amellia broke into a blues number that she had written herself, the crew were absolutely astounded, they had spent most of the time that they had been working for Power-man productions listening to karaoke singers that could not even hold a note, now standing before them was a unique talent, in the same league as the late Amy Winehouse.

When she finished Mellissa applauded and said 'Amellia that was amazing, you really do have something special, I am sure you will go far, very far.'

Powell just sat there with his arms folded across his chest in an attempt to look as disinterested as he possibly could. Then he gave his verdict in the most belittling manner 'Amellia sweet sweet Amellia, you will go about as far as the old people's home you have no career in show-business now get out of here and stop wasting my time.'

The twinkle in the eye of the young vocalist disappeared as the sweet look of pure innocence instantly turned to one of sheer rage, as she yelled back at him 'I don't give a shit about old people, all they do is sit around all day pissing themselves. I only said that I liked them, so that you would like me and put me on your show. The truth is I left home when I was fourteen and have been living in a squat and dealing drugs ever since. So you can stick your show right up your arse.'

As Amellia was ranting the big fat ugly bully (Presumably Powell's bodyguard) that had been standing out of the camera shot started walking towards her in a menacing way. As Powell quickly rose from his seat he gestured with his right hand for him to back off. Mellissa held her head in her hands feeling that she would feel the wrath of Powell for that outburst.

What followed next came as a total shock to her and everyone on the set. Amellia had turned to leave the studio, but Powell stopped her by yelling 'Hold on, what did you just say?'

Without hesitation Amellia pointed at him as she yelled back 'I said you can stick your show right up your arse.'

'No before that.'

'Old people just sit around all day pissing themselves.'

'No after that.'

Amellia became inquisitive, she was surprised that Powell was now interested, her face and tone of voice changed 'You mean living in a squat and dealing drugs?'

'Yes tell me about that. How did that happen?'

'Well I was seeing this boy, it started when he came to my fourteenth birthday party, all the girls had the hot's for him, he had a really wicked car with a well cool sound system, and well my parents didn't like it, they said I was too young to be having that type of relationship, my dad said he was going to kill him. They stopped me from going out at night, so one day I bunked off school and moved into a squat with my boyfriend and his mates.'

'Apart from you being fourteen, was there any other reason why you think your parents didn't want you seeing this boy?'

The animosity between the two of them had gone, the crew were surprised to see that for the first time ever Powell seemed to be taking a genuine interest in one of the show's potential participants that he had just seconds before dismissed.

Amellia was curious as to why he was showing such an interest in her personal life, but she carried on speaking frankly 'I dunno really, I'm not sure whether it was because my dad was being racist, or if it was because my boyfriend was a dealer and he was older than me.'

'So how old was this boy? And what exactly was he dealing?'

'He was ten years older than me, twenty four he was, and he was dealing in all sorts E's, Crack, H the lot, anything he could get hold of. I use to help him out a bit, but I never touched the gear myself apart from a bit of puff, that other shit kills people.'

This was not entirely true, Amellia had taken any drug that had been offered to her, but it was cannabis that she smoked on a regular basis.

Powell was now more than just a little bit interested in her relationship with her drug dealer boyfriend. He asked 'What else can you tell me about your boyfriend? What is he doing now?'

'He's dead! Somebody shot him, lucky I weren't with him at the time, I had already left him and gone off with one of his mates. I thought he was the one, he was real cool and boy could he rap, and he knew how to dress, but then he started slapping me about, so I fucked off.'

'Where are you living now?'

'Well I had to move out of London, it was getting too dangerous, everyone I knew was carrying guns and knives, I heard a few of them wanted to do me in. So I moved to Milton Keynes with a boy I knew from school, it's a bit of a shithole but at least it's safe and we're the only dealers in our street.'

Mellissa decided to join in the conversation, she was concerned for the young girl and the situation she lived in.

Her concern was apparent by the tone of her voice 'What about your parents? Have you contacted them? They must be worried sick.'

'No I haven't spoken to them since I left home, I changed my mobile number and I got off of face-book and twitter. They were looking for me see, they put me on the missing persons list, it was all over the radio and it was in all the newspapers, but they'll get over it.'

'But you should contact your parents, to let them know where you are. At least let them know that you are OK.'

Powell was irritated by Mellissa's interruption, he had not invited her to voice her opinion. If ever he needed confirmation that the only reason that he had employed her was because she was a great piece of arse it was now. Standing before him was an eighteen year old girl that had already attracted the interest of the media and she could not see the benefit. He lifted his hand to Mellissa's face to gesture for her to shut up. When he spoke it was with a friendly enthusiastic tone 'Amellia, what if I get a camera crew to go back to your squat with you now? What would you say if I tell you they will interview for the show today, and I will definitely put you on my show? The Factor?

'That's wicked.'

'And if you really impress me I might even give you a recording contract.'

'Oh wicked.'

'I'll arrange for a car to take you back now.'

A massive smile beamed across Amellia's face. As she turned to leave she praised Powell with the words 'Ah thanks I didn't mean what I said earlier, you're the man, you're sick.'

As Amellia left the studio Mellissa turned to Powell and asked. 'Do you think we should notify the girl's parents, they must be distraught?'

'Don't be stupid this is exactly what the show needs.'

'But I think we should at least tell her parents where she is, they must be worried out of their minds.'

'But you think, but you think, if I wanted somebody that could think I would not have employed you. I would have hired a man. Now we say nothing, I will put her on the show, somebody that knows her family is bound to recognize her when she appears on television and contact her parents. The newspapers and radio stations are notified, and I am the lovely person that that gave her the chance to make something of her life and reunited her with her parents and her two little brothers. It's a winner.'

'Is she going to be the winner?'

'No I've already sorted that, but she'll get through to the finals and we'll have a camera on her parents as they sit there in the auditorium amongst the audience choking back the tears. Maybe this is the answer, maybe we have overdone the nice girl image. Maybe we need the rebellious type I reckon I have found the answer, no more mister nice guy. And no more snivelling bitches.'

Too Nice

"Keep your friends close and your enemies closer."
Is a quotation from a well-known mafia film that we are
all familiar with.
Powell never had any friends, well not what one would
describe as friends in the conventional way.
 A normal person would describe a friend as somebody
that they mutually enjoyed the company of.
Or maybe a person that lived on the other side of the world
that they did not see from one year to the next but was
only as far as a telephone call away.
 Powell had nobody in his life like that. Although he had
what one would describe as hangers on. There were a few
people that felt that being associated with him meant some
of his fame and fortune would rub off on them, but none
of them actually liked anything about him as a person.
And neither of them could relate to him in anyway, they
just nodded in agreement when he spoke and forced a

laugh at his jokes, even-though they found his perverse sense of humour quite sickening.

There was only one person that he had anything in common with. Only one person that he could connect with in anyway. A man that he saw as his equal.

That man was fellow television presenter Jezza Lyle.

He begrudgingly admired the way Lyle manipulated the viewing public.

Like himself Lyle had no talent whatsoever, and absolutely nothing likeable about his personality.

He was extremely arrogant and did not have two brain cells to rub together. To say he lacked morals would be an understatement, the word "Moral" did not feature in his dictionary, but somehow he managed to manipulate television audiences on both sides of the Atlantic.

The words his associate Lyle had uttered to him when the viewing figures of The Factor had dropped by a significant amount were still ringing through his head.

"You know what your problem is you're too nice. And the members of the public that you have on your show they are too nice as well. Now that is not what the television audiences want to see, no, they want to see people that are worse than them, people that they can look down their noses at. Picture this. A hundred thousand women that are living in the U.K are shagging their husband's brother. So what do they do? I'll tell you what they do, they tune in to my show, because they want to see some filthy disgusting bitch shagging her husband's father. It makes them feel good about themselves. Hundreds of thousands of people take illegal un-prescribed drugs, so they tune in to my show to see the heroin addicts. It's not rocket science, they don't want to see nice people. And do you know what your problem is? You're too nice as well. Now look at me. I don't take any nonsense do I? I tell them "It's the Jezza Lyle show. It's the Jezza Lyle show." So drop the nice guy image and get society's low-life's on your show, otherwise you will become one of television's old has beens by the time you're sixty."

This was not what Powell wanted to hear.

He had found the formula to get the masses tuning in, but it was not working anymore.

Lyle had managed to keep himself on national television every single day for the past fourteen years both here in the United Kingdom and The United States of America. Based solely on the theory that people only want to see the worst in other people in order to be able to feel good about themselves.

Despite the fact that the only reward Lyle had ever given to the members of the public that appeared on his show was a night in a tacky hotel he had an enormous amount of lowlife's that would do anything to appear on television and announce to the nation that they feel that. "It is wrong for my boyfriend to be shagging my sister! And just because I am not sure whether or not the baby I had three months ago is his or one of the local rugby players that is no excuse."

And why they wanted to inform the entire nation that they had never done an honest day's work because the social security pays for their upkeep was totally beyond him. In order to secure a place on the Jezza Lyle show, there were people that had their teeth pulled out, or stained a shitty brown colour, whilst others had ugly looking tattoo's drawn on their necks and foreheads.

He even had a Christmas celebrity special featuring C list celebrities doing their dirty washing in public.

One of the shows featured an over the hill topless model with false tits and a Botox face claiming that her husband liked to dress up in women's clothing, while she strapped on a dildo and performed anal sex on him. It was a smash hit with the audience as he stringently denied it until she pulled out photographic evidence.

Lyle did not even need to be thinking of new idea's to keep the show alive. The story was always the same.

He did not need to have a team of researchers sifting through countless applications to appear on his show, anybody with an ounce of self-respect would not dream of washing their dirty linen in public. Therefore only suitable shameless candidates ever applied, all the crew needed to do was encourage them to behave in the most undignified, disgraceful manner that they possibly would when they found themselves in front of the camera.

So maybe that is what The Factor needs, it's had plenty of what Powell himself referred to as misfits, the sort of people that you wouldn't want to meet as you go about your daily business, but you quite happily sat back in the comfort of your own home and laughed at.

So maybe Lyle is right. Maybe The Factor need's society's vermin, maybe it needs people that have no respect for themselves or anybody else.

But how many people that looked as though they have never washed, with hair that looked like it was home to half the population of insect life and had rotten teeth, had countless amounts of children with different partners in order to claim more social security benefit and was a drug addict with a sexually transmitted disease, wanted to make a career in show-business?

Powell thought about this deeply. If I could get the participants of my show to show a darker side to their character, if I could get them to publicly announce all of their wrong doings and talk about their sexual indiscretions, and any immoral or illegal activities that they have participated in, then maybe just maybe my show will be back on top.

That must be the answer, I've exhausted every other idea, it must be the answer.

The Beautiful Twins

Mellissa picked up the blue plastic clipboard that she had placed on the oblong table in front of her and began to read from her notes. 'We have a story here that I think the audience will love. It's a boy/girl singing duo they're brother and sister, twins to be precise. Their parents were killed in a car crash when they were just eleven years old. They have no other relatives as neither of their parents had any brothers or sisters. So they were brought up in care homes. They never had the chance to settle anywhere. When they were thirteen social services placed them in separate foster homes but after two weeks the boy Sebastian became very ill, I do not know what the illness was, that has not been specified but I know Sebastian has special needs and has difficulty coping with certain situations, it was felt that he could not be without his sister, so they were never separated again. Now they are twenty one years of age and they are living in a small rented flat in Bedfordshire. Neither one of them are in employment but they practice singing together every day and they are hoping to make a career in show business. I read their story and I met up with them, they are amazing. Seeing them together brought tears to my eyes, they are just so sweet, you should see the way Sebastian looks at his sister Mary-Anne, I have never seen such a genuine, sincere look of love in a person's eyes before, they absolutely adore each other and you can see he would be totally lost without her, it's so touching. The audience will really take them to their hearts, I am sure of it.'

Powell did not like what he was hearing at all, they had had far too many sympathy cases. Which was why according to the researchers the viewing figures had dropped. Almost every other person that appeared on his show had claimed to have been bullied at school, then there were the ones that had terminal illnesses, he had had an enormous amount of people that had lost someone they loved dearly to a terrible disease, then there were the characters that did not fit into society at all but claimed that it was their singing that managed to get them through life. But no more sympathy, it had been done to death. Shaking his head he sternly replied. 'No, no that won't work, we have over done it with the sympathy. My show needs a new angle. Never forget it is all about the ratings.'

'But they look so good together, Mary-Anne is really pretty, in fact she is absolutely gorgeous and he has this little boy lost look about him, with those big blue puppy dog eyes. They both have beautiful blue eyes.'

Suddenly something triggered Powell's interest. 'Describe the girl, to me, what does she look like?'

'She is absolutely beautiful with a figure to die for. Mary-Anne could easily make a career as a glamour model. If you are looking for eye candy, she is perfect.'

'And did you say the lad is retarded?'

'He has special needs.'

'Special needs, of course, that's what they call it these days. So tell me about the boy with special needs.'

A beaming smile came across Mellissa's face and the twinkle returned to her eye as she spoke of the young lad that she had the pleasure of meeting a few weeks previously. 'He's ever so sweet, and he's always holding his sister Mary-Anne's hand and he speaks with such a soft voice. Sebastian has that look that makes you want to hug him. I'm sure when the ladies see him they will fall for him, he's adorable. The twins are sitting in the green room now, would you like to see them?'

Powell did not answer he just gave an approving nod.

Mellissa lifted the handset pushed the button and said 'Number four thousand eight hundred and forty one Sebastian and Mary-Anne.'

Powell stood up and began to pace the floor as he asked. 'If you were a man, on a scale of one to ten, one being I wouldn't touch her with a barge pole and ten being, I could totally shag the arse of her. What score would you give this girl Carrie-Anne?'

Mellissa felt uncomfortable, she felt the colour in her face go deep red.

The studio was silent, Powell was looking at her expecting an answer. Everybody in the studio could sense her discomfort.

Mellissa knew she had to answer, but she could not look anyone in the eye, she bowed her head and answered.

'Ten.'

'Perfect, her shag-ability is a ten. I will put them on The Factor. What we will do is show a two minute clip of them at home together, we get the point across to the viewing public that he is totally dependent on his sister, we let the audience see that ever since their parents were killed they have been completely devoted to each other. Do you like it so far?'

Powell often asked for approval from his employee's when he came up with an idea, despite the fact that they knew not to disagree with him.

If their view was contrary to his they kept it to themselves. They knew if they openly disapproved of his ideas he would ridicule them and they could face the prospect of losing their job.

'Yes it makes a really touching story, I'm sure the audience will love them.'

Having got the answer he expected to get Powell carried on. 'Then we hear them sing, we choose a song for them that really shows their bond for each other, like they could not live for one moment without each other, you weep, the audience weep, then as you are wiping the tears from your eyes you advise the girl, Carrie-Anne'

'Mary-Anne.'

'Mary-Anne, I like that name it has a religious feel to it. You look at Mary-Anne through your tear stained eyes and you tell her that. That was the most beautiful thing you have ever heard, that she has real talent, but her brother is holding her back and you feel that you can only put her through to the next round if she agrees to ditch him and go solo. I will agree with you, then we get her to tell her brother that she loves him, but feels that she must pursue her career. If he breaks down in tears that would be perfect. She leaves him to go to boot camp.

We then get her posing topless for the tabloid papers.

We then leak it to the press that she is now living the high life, out clubbing every night, wearing designer clothes and sleeping around, don't forget to mention that she is on her way to her first recording contract, whilst her sweet twin brother is being cared for in hospital with severe depression. The media will love it.'

Mellissa did not like this. She asked. 'What about Sebastian?'

'What?'

'Sebastian, if Mary-Anne ditches him, I don't think he will be able to cope, he has never spent a day without her he absolutely adores her.'

'That's right that is the whole point, with Sebastian having a complete breakdown, whilst his sister is out there living the high life, the press will not be able to leave it alone.'

'I really don't think we should do that, it could be very damaging for Sebastian.'

'I have just come up with a plan to re-ignite my show, to boost viewing figures and all you can say is "What about Sebastian?" I'll tell you what about Sebastian, I don't give a shit about Sebastian and if you give a shit about your own career, you won't give a shit about Sebastian either.

If I decide to put them on my show, I will decide what we do about Sebastian.'

Jason the camera man coughed loudly then he called out. 'Hello darlings, we've been waiting for you.'

That was very tactful of him, as Powell stopped his ranting and looked towards the entrance to the studio.

Nicola lead Mary-Anne and Sebastian to the spot in which they were to stand before Powell as she did so Nicola announced. 'Mary-Anne and Sebastian number four thousand eight hundred and forty one.'

Powell eyed Mary-Anne up and down, Mellissa was right this girl really was a stunner, she scored top marks on the shag-ability scale.

He would have no problem in getting her pics plastered all over the lad's mags as well as the tabloids.

Whilst Powell was ogling the glamorous young lady in front of him, Mellissa said. 'Can you tell us a little bit about yourselves and what you are going to do for us today?'

'My names Mary-Anne and this is my brother Sebastian. Today we are going to sing for you.'

'Would you like to tell us about your hobbies? What do you do in your spare time? And when did you both start singing?'

'Oh yes of course. Sebastian likes trains, we go to the train station regularly, and we sit by the side of the railway line and watch the trains as they pass, and sometimes we take a packed lunch. Sebastian likes in when we have a picnic. We also like walking and we spend a lot of time in the park, the keeper threw us off the swings yesterday, he said "You are too big to be playing on those, you should act your age." So we just ran off, it was so funny, we could not stop laughing.'

'That is funny. Can you tell us about the singing? When did you first start singing together?'

'We have been singing together for the whole of our lives, we sing every day, our mother said she heard us singing in the womb. Do you remember that Sebastian?'

Sebastian nervously replied in almost a whisper 'Yes we do everything together.'

'Oh that is sweet.' Mellissa replied with a big friendly smile 'And what are you going to sing for us today?'

'We are going to sing a song that we have wrote ourselves, it's called. Together we can make it.'

'Go on then, good luck.'

The twins took a deep breath and sung.

At times when things are difficult
And it's hard to carry on
But because we've got each other
We know we can't go wrong
We can walk the earth together
We can climb the highest high
We can swim the widest ocean
We can fly up to the sky

The sound was so dreadful the only way I can explain it would be to say that if you took a dozen cats and simultaneously castrated them with blunt knives whilst they were wide awake with nothing whatsoever to ease the pain, it would still not be possible for it to sound that bad. They were completely tone deaf.

Powell cut in, he stood up with a massively big friendly smile across his face. 'That's enough. That is enough, I don't need to hear anymore. You two are on the show. Sebastian your sister Carrie-Anne.'

'Mary-Anne my sister's name is Mary-Anne.'

'Of course Mary-Anne, she's very pretty isn't she? If I ran away with her, to some far away land, forever and ever, would that be Okay with you?'

Sebastian did not like what he was hearing, his jaw dropped and his bottom lip began to quiver as he shook his head and replied. 'No'

'I'm only jesting Sebastian, I'm not going to run away with your sister, but can Mellissa have a girly chat with her while we have a man to man? Now you see Sebastian, what will happen is you are going to be on television and you will make lots of money, have you ever had a job?'

'No but I had an interview last week for a job in a supermarket collecting the trolleys, I am waiting to hear from them to see if I've got it.'

Whilst Powell and Sebastian were chatting Mellissa took Mary-Anne to one side to speak with her. 'So are you excited?'

'Yes very much, if our singing career takes off, it will be amazing for Sebastian I know he will love it.'

'A little tip, when you are on the show, whatever we say to you just nod and agree with it, it might not seem to make sense at the time, but trust me the whole picture works out well and makes sense in the end.'

Powell held out his hands as he addressed the twins. 'So that's it, you are both going to be on the television and you will make lots of money. Mellissa will give you the full info and I will see you on my show.'

Mellissa gave them both a cheery smile as she spoke. 'Bye bye for now, I have your address and telephone number, we will contact you with more details.'

'The twins thanked them and left the studio happily holding hands.

As the door closed behind them the smile on Mellissa's face dropped as she turned to Powell apologetically. 'I am so sorry this is the first time that I have ever heard them sing, I never imagined they would   be so bad.'

'Who cares about how they sing? They will look good on my show. And you were right she is a little cracker, well shag-able, I might even give her a portion myself. I want extra attention paid to the way she is dressed, I want to see every single bump and curve, make the skirt as short as possible and all of her tops must be low cut, I want to see lots of cleavage, that girls got gorgeous tits let's put them on display. I cannot wait for the moment when our glamour model tells her poor backward brother that is totally dependent on her that she is ditching him and will be singing solo. Despite the fact that we have well over done it with the sympathy pitch, this has got the makings of a real winner, when he breaks down because his callous self-centred bitch of a sister has decided to leave him for her own selfish reasons, the public will hate her.'

Mellissa did not like Powell's scheme and so she tried to reason with him. 'But she is not a glamour model. And do you really think it is right for us to split them up?'

'She will be glamour model, I will make her into one. You said yourself. "She could easily make a career as a glamour model." And I don't think I know if we can make it look like she has totally cast her brother aside to become a pop star and is out there living the high life whilst he is on the brink of suicide, it will put us back on the front pages. The public will be tuning in by the millions to see the dirty little slut that ditched her poor defenceless brother. What is good for my show is right.'

Mellissa did not like it one little bit, but she felt that if she didn't protest too loudly then maybe Powell may decide on a different course of action for the twins, because after all they were the ultimate eye candy and they both had the most beautiful eyes that were absolutely identical. She felt that keeping them together was the best way to use the twins and hoped that Powell would see it that way as well.

George Answell

The time was now 4.30 pm and Powell was not happy he had auditioned dozens of hopefuls and there were only a handful that he felt he could use on his show.

He looked towards Mellissa and barked. 'This is just not good enough, today has been a complete waste of my time. Show me something of interest.'

Mellissa sensing Powell's frustration replied nervously. 'Next in line we have a man who's extremely keen and' Powell cut in 'They're all extremely keen, now come on, stop wasting my time, just get them in here.'

Nicola entered the studio followed by a gentleman dressed in casual everyday clothing following behind her.

She instructed him to 'Stand on the cross and look into the camera.'

Mellissa welcomed him in her usual friendly manner and said. 'Before you start, can you tell us a little bit about yourself?'

The man answered very slowly and kept pausing midsentence. 'Well my name is George Answell. I'm fifty four years old. And I have been working. Excuse me I'm a bit nervous. As a delivery driver in London. For the past three and a half years.'

Due to the unnecessary pausing it had taken him what seemed to Powell as an eternity to introduce himself.

This irritated Powell, as sarcastically as he possibly could he remarked. 'How interesting, I'm going to wet myself with excitement.'

'What are you going to sing for us today?' Asked Mellissa.

'Well I would like to sing you a song, if that's okay? This song reminds me of my younger years and it's something quite special to me.'

The man then sang an old classic from the 1960's his voice was amazing, the entire crew were in awe.

He had to be the best singer that had ever auditioned for The Factor.

Mellissa's eyes widened as the pitch perfect voice delivered the song with so much compassion.

Powell was not impressed, and he wanted to show it, he spoke to George Answell in the most belittling tone that he possibly could. 'Why oh! Why would anyone be interested in a fifty four year old delivery driver? You have got about as much personality and appeal as a politician at a train spotter's convention dear man. Now get out of here and go and deliver whatever it is that you deliver.'

As George turned to walk away Powell carried on not bothered that he was still within earshot. 'What a bloody waste of time he was. In fact the whole of today has been a waste of time. Let's end it now and come back Wednesday.'

'But Mister Powell' Said Mellissa. There are still a lot of people waiting to see you.'

'Tell them to come back Wednesday, I have had enough for today and I'm not here tomorrow.'

The crew were sickened by the treatment George Answell had received and equally sickened that the people that had waited all day to be auditioned were now going to be turned away. But everyone knew that it would be senseless to protest.

Misfits

It was 10.45 on Wednesday morning when Powell strolled into the studio.

The crew were there ready and waiting to begin.

The green room was packed with people hoping that today was their day, the first step to a new life.

Powell never acknowledged any of the crew, his first words were 'Coffee.' An instruction for somebody to fetch him a drink.

He then looked at Mellissa and stated. 'Today I want to see the misfits.'

Powell knew that in the days when his talent shows were successful it was largely as a result of the misfits, people that did not seem to fit into society, that were totally void of ant talent whatsoever, but for some strange reason they actually believed that they could make a career in show-business. It was them, the misfits, they had made him a success. They were the eccentrics that the viewing public tuned in to see. And even though he would never have admitted it to anyone, he knew his show would never have taken off in the first instance without them.

He recalled the numerous amount of auditionee's that could not sing a note, but would shamelessly strip to their underwear as they belted out a song.

He had a vivid recollection of all the foul mouthed wannabee's that swore at him and his crew and made abusive remarks when they were publicly rejected.

Then there were the endless stream of emotional cry-babies that would burst into floods of tears for no apparent reason. Not to forget the countless amount of people that simply looked ridiculous because they simply had no dress sense whatsoever.

They were what the majority of viewers had tuned in to see, hence the reason why he looked at Mellissa and said. 'Tell me about the misfits.'

As she was looking at the notes on her clipboard, his pretty young assistant replied 'We have the usual amount of people that think they can sing, but are completely tone deaf. Loads of dancers, some are quite good they can move but most don't even feel the beat of the music.'

'We always have an abundance of those.' Powell retorted. 'But do we have any freakishly wacky characters? Do we have men with breasts? Or women with beards? It might not be a bad idea to have a few animals on the show. They were once good for viewing figures. Get the crew too sort through the animals. I don't suppose you would remember the three legged dog that walked the tightrope, would you? And what about the lowlifes that people would find absolutely disgusting, like the bloke that actually thought he could make a career by drinking fizzy drinks and burping into the microphone. Do we have many applicants like that?'

Mellissa looked through her notes. 'We have the usual amount of I need to get a life brigade, you know the people that think they will find fame and fortune by setting light to their own farts.'

Powell shook his head in a manner that you may have thought was disbelief, but he did not disbelieve it, he had known from the very beginning that there was an endless amount of people willing to put all sense of self respect and dignity aside to appear on national television.

As he shook his head he stated. 'We have had a fart lighter on the show before, right at the beginning, let's do it again let us have another fart lighter, we'll go for the one that looks the most ridiculous.'

'We have one that wears a homemade Superman outfit.' Answered Mellissa enthusiastically.

'He'll do, there's no need for me to audition him, get one of the crew to tell him he's on the show.' Said Powell. 'What other freaks have we got?'

'This one looks interesting, we have a man that plays a tune by blowing down the spout of a watering can.'

'What tune does he play?'

'Land of hope and glory.'

'How long do you think he would last before the audience booed him off?'

'I would guess a few seconds at the most.'

'I would expect that, somebody tell him he's on the show. What else have we got?'

'We have got one guy that really does seem like a bit of an odd one, he doesn't really have much of a story to tell, he is very much an introvert, he told us that he doesn't have any friends or hobbies and that he has never been in a relationship, he also says, and I quote "My ambition is to meet a nice girl and get married." For an act he can put twenty two marsh mellows in his mouth whilst saying "Fluffy bunnies." Would you like to see him?'

'Yes I think I can make something of his case, I will see him today.' Replied Powell.

Then he looked at Mellissa and said. 'I don't suppose you are old enough to remember the fifty year old virgin I had on the show, she had never done a thing with her life, she was born and brought up in a quiet little village in the arse end of nowhere, so apart from that had no story to tell. She had facial hair and stubble on her chin, she also looked like she was growing a moustache, but she had the voice of an angel. I made a pretty penny from her and she increased the ratings. I wish we had a few more like that. Do we have anyone like her?'

The fifty year old virgin that Powell had referred too also did more for his image and the image of The Factor than all of his marketing experts had ever done put together. The whole nation warmed to the sweet innocent lady that up until the moment when she took her first steps onto the stage and blew the entire viewing audience away with an amazing voice that did not seem to match her appearance had lead a very humble life. Millions of people tuned in to see this lovable character. Then he Trenton Powell gave her a recording contract and put her onto the world famous London Palladium stage, where she sang in front of the Queen on The Royal Variety Show.

For a short while some people actually saw Powell as a good man. They forgot about the hundreds people that he had publicly humiliated on national television.

'No but we do have a long list of odd characters.' Replied Mellissa.

For the next twenty minutes she read through the long list of strange characters that were waiting in the large cold hall which Powell called "The green room."

So that was that, Powell instructed his floorwalkers to send everyone away that he did not class as a misfit.

They were to come back the following morning.

Today he would concentrate on misfits.

The first person to follow Nicola through the studio doors, was a sweet looking little old lady. She was very tiny and even though she looked quite fragile, she had quite a spring in her step.

The best way I could possibly describe her would be by saying, if you wanted somebody to play the role of the sweetest, lovable grandmother ever, then she would be your girl.

Mellissa instantly warmed to her and greeted her with 'Hello it's nice to see you here. Can you tell us a little bit about yourself? And what you are going to do for us today?'

When she spoke the sweet little old lady had the softest voice ever. 'My name is Dorothy, but everybody calls me "Dolly" I'm ninety two years young and I help out at the local hospice, as a volunteer. I also make cakes to sell at the village fetes to raise money for the homeless.'

'That's lovely.' Said Mellissa. 'And what are you going to do today for your audition?'

'I am going to sing a song that I would like to dedicate to my late husband Archie. We were married for sixty two

years before God took him from me and into his home.'
Dolly then sang the sweetest of love songs.
Tears flowed from Mellissa's eyes.
When Dolly finished Mellissa said. 'You sang that song
beautifully. You have a smile that could brighten the
dullest day. You really are the sweetest person we have
ever had audition for the show. I love you and I am sure
the viewing audience will love you also.'
Powell was not pleased, he had already made it clear that
he did not want any more sweet sickly characters, he had
just minutes before stated that he wanted to devote today
to the misfits. He decided to take his anger out on Dolly.
Shaking his head slowly from side to side he said. 'If this
was a sweet little old lady competition, you would win it
hands down I am sure of it. But The Factor is all about
finding the stars of the future. You have not got what it
takes to be a star. You have just wasted five minutes of my
time and to be perfectly honest you don't look to me as if
you have a future either.'
'That's because you're a cunt.' The sweet old lady said as
she turned to exit the studio.
The crew found this hilarious and were biting themselves
to prevent themselves from laughing out loud.
Sensing Powell was not a happy bunny. Jason called out
'Let's take a break Darlings.' Then walked over to Powell
and taking him by the arm said. 'I bet you have not eaten
today, come on let's have brunch.'

Too Fat

The grieving father looked through tearstained eyes at the 10x8 colour photograph of his only child.

The picture showed a very pretty, bright, bubbly eighteen year old girl that had a real zest for life, and great expectations for the future.

Natasha was popular with everyone she met, always greeting her friends and her father with a warm hug.

At school she scored well above the national average on every subject. Her greatest love, was what she really excelled at music. She wanted to follow in her father's footsteps and make a career as an opera singer.

Her father was born and raised in England but was best known in Italy where he performed many times at the world famous opera house La Scala in Milan.

When Natasha was just seven years old her mother was diagnosed with cancer.

Her father quit singing to care for her, then when she passed away, he quit singing and brought his daughter up himself and never returned to the stage.

 The bond between Natasha and her dad was strong he supported her in everything she did and paid for her to have private vocal lesson's. Her voice had an extraordinary wide range and he was sure that she had a promising career ahead of her.

He tried to persuade her not to partake in a television talent show, but when she said. "But Daddy this is what I really want, more than anything else." He replied "I wish for you everything that you wish for yourself."

With her father's blessing Natasha's auditioned and was successful, at that time she was exactly the type of person that the show's researchers were looking for.

When they had told her that she had made it to the live show and would be appearing on national television she was delighted.

On the day of the show there were in excess of twenty thousand people in the audience and Trenton Powell along with three other judges were present.

Away from the crowds and the focus of the cameras Natasha was told by one of the Power-Man researchers. "You really have got The Factor, and you are just one step away from a recording contract. So go out there and show the world what you can do. This is the first day of the rest of your life."

When she sang the audience were silent, I swear they even stopped breathing, such was the effect of hearing Natasha's incredible voice. When she finished the applause was deafening.

The applause faded, a camera was focused on Natasha's expression of real happiness, she was thrilled that her performance had received such an appreciative response from the live audience.

A camera was also focused on Powell. He did not look as enthusiastic as anybody else as he said. 'The ability to sing is not enough, appearance is important for a performing artist. I am looking for potential recording stars that look and sound exceptional, and you I'm afraid are just too plump. So it's a big fat no from me, and I am sure the others will agree.'

The others did not agree, but as Powell said it he scratched his right ear lobe which they knew was the sign to follow whatever he said.

They nodded their heads in unison and made comments like. "You need to lose a bit of weight."

"Maybe you should come back when you are slimmer."

Natasha was not overweight. She was also not skinny. She had a healthy well-proportioned figure, but Powell had told her that she was plump in the hope of getting the reaction that he wanted.

And he was not disappointed. Natasha stood there on the vast stage with a camera zoomed into her face and sobbed uncontrollably.

This was shown to millions of television viewers and the daily tabloid newspapers also picked up on it. With one of them making it their headlining story.

"Factor Contestant Sobs. I'm Too Fat"

Below the headline was a picture of an eighteen year old girl with the make-up that the Power-man team had applied to her running down her face as she sobbed her heart out.

Powell was delighted, this kind of publicity could only be good for increasing viewing figures.

It did not occur to him for one second that it did nothing to boost his personal popularity. Besides he would not have noticed any change, due to his arrogance and his callous behaviour towards others, he had been disliked for his entire life.

A few days after her feature in the tabloid's Natasha was approached by a man, who said. "I'm sure you have heard of me everybody who is anybody in show business has heard of me." He then went on to show her photographs of himself with some well-known faces from the entertainment industry.

He told her "I was Lionel Ritchie's promoter and Marvin Gaye's. Do you know when Marvin's father shot him dead I was the first person they notified?"

He then said. "I would like to manage you and get you in the recording studio, I will book a world tour to promote your first album, starting with your own show at the world famous London Palladium to launch your career. I will get a famous friend of mine to be your support act, he owes me a favour. We will invite all the showbiz stars, it will be a massive gala night. They all know me. It was me that put Phil Collins on the plane."

Natasha was thrilled. Who wouldn't be? She was still aching from the humiliation of being reduced to tears on national television but things were looking up and in the future Powell's callous treatment of her would become a distant memory.

She was given a date for her show at The Palladium and was told by the promoter to "Announce the good news and promote the show on the social networking sites."

She did what she was instructed to do and she contacted her local newspaper, they published a picture of her standing outside the Palladium with her hands in the air in jubilation. With the headlines

Local Singer All Set To Hit the Big Time

The excitement was overwhelming, her friends were buying V.I.P advance tickets from the promoter.

Then five days after the feature in her local newspaper, her promoter called at her home when her father was out, he told her. "We have hit a snag. The Palladium have contacted me and said another show producer wants to book the space the very Sunday night that we are booked in for and unless we can come up with a £12,000 deposit today, we will lose our chance at The Palladium. I have got tens of thousands of pounds tied up in a big tour that I was telling you about, so I have a cash flow problem. I'm sorry but it looks like your gala night at the famous London Palladium is off"

Natasha had £10,000 in a trust fund that her mother had left her, she told the producer "I have £10,000 that my mum left me in her will, I can get that, but what about the other £2,000?" He smiled and put his hand on her knee, as he was gently rubbing he said. "I may have a cash flow problem but I am not a pauper, £2,000 is petty cash to me, I can add that to your £10,000 and The London Palladium is all yours."

Natasha transferred her £10,000 into his bank account and she never heard from him again.

The realisation that she had been conned along with the humiliation she felt for unwittingly assisting him in conning her friends to buy tickets for a none existent show became too much for her, she became very withdrawn. Prior to her appearance on The Factor she had a very healthy social life and a wide circle of genuine friends. Her friends became concerned, they tried their very best to be supportive, but whenever they tried to call her, she did not answer her phone. Neither did she reply to any message they had left for her via text, email or social media. When they called at the home she shared with her father, she refused to see them.

Natasha locked herself in her bedroom, she did not wish to interact with anybody. Even her own father that had as close a bond that any man could have with his daughter felt as if he had been shut out of her life.

Natasha's appearance changed drastically. She rapidly lost weight, her once full of life bouncy hair became thin and lifeless and her shiny bright skin became dull and pale.

As he looked through tear stained eyes at the photograph of his dearly departed little girl, the loving father vowed revenge.

Tourette's

It was 1.15pm when Jason and Powell returned from brunch, the whole morning had passed and apart from the sweet little old lady that Powell had rejected, nobody waiting in the vast hall, the "Green room" had been auditioned that day.

As he returned to his seat, addressing the whole of the crew Powell said. 'I haven't got time to waste so for the remainder of the day, I want to see them in here quickly, so come on let's move it.'

First through the studio doors was a rather average looking man in his mid-thirties, he was clean shaven and dressed in a very smart suit with a double breasted jacket, and a clean white crisp shirt.

Powell shook his head and tutted. He had ordered misfits but there seemed to be nothing odd about him, apart from the black eye that he was sporting.

It was Mellissa that spoke first. 'Can you tell us your name and what you are going to do for us today?'

'Slut.' Was the reply she received.

Mellissa did not like that, she sat upright in her chair as she asked. 'I beg your pardon?'

'Slut.'

Nicola interjected 'His name is Lawrence and he has Tourette's. That is why he has a black eye a man thought that he was insulting his wife.'

'Stupid prick.' Said Lawrence.

Now that Mellissa understood she was no longer offended. And her caring nature came through. 'I understand Lawrence, I have read about Tourette's and how it effects the people that suffer with it, I can so much sympathies with you. If only more people understood your condition you would not have to encounter so much prejudice.'

'Silly Slut.'

Powell liked this, he found it very amusing hearing Mellissa being called a "Slut."

He also felt that he would be a big hit with the viewing audience. They had never had a Tourette's sufferer on The Factor before. Whatever this man did for an act he was certainly going to be on the show.

Mellissa asked again. 'So Lawrence what are you going to do for your audition?'

He did not answer, he just burst into a classic swing number made famous by the late Tony Bennett.

I would describe the way Lawrence sang as being slightly off key, certainly not good enough to make a career on the variety circuit.

When he finished Mellissa applauded him. Then when she spoke his condition could not stop him from interrupting.

'I can so much sympathies with you'

'Slut.'

'But you do not seem to hear the key'

'Fucking Whore.'

'Have you thought about taking singing lessons?'

'Slut.'

'I so much sympathies with your condition, but The Factor is a family show and I do not feel that you are suitable.'
'Fucking Slag.'
Mellissa was visibly upset. She had tried to empathize with Lawrence, although despite her caring nature she really did not appreciate being insulted in this manner.
On the other hand Powell thought it was highly amusing, he was holding his stomach as he was rocking back and forth laughing.
When he did manage to compose himself he told Lawrence 'I do not feel that your condition should in anyway affect your chances of taking part in The Factor. Power-man productions is an equal opportunities employer, so therefore you Lawrence have past the audition and I will be seeing you on the live show.'

In the year 2025 foul language is now acceptable on National television regardless of the time it is being shown.
There is no longer such a thing as The Watershed. Although it is no longer acceptable to refer to a Scotsman as "Jock" or an Irishman as "Paddy."
A year previously a comedian called a Welshman in the audience "Taffy" he was taken to court and fined £25,000. He refused to pay.
His words to the judge were. "I refuse to pay a single penny. How out of touch with the real world are you? My best friend comes from Cardiff, I call him Taffy all the

time and he does not take Offence. Taffy is also black, would you prefer it if I called him Nigger?"

The comedian got sentenced to three months in prison for contempt of court and a further three months for racism.

The previous day a participant on the Jezza Lyle show called her ex-lover a "Dirty lying cheating Cunt" and nobody batted an eyelid despite the fact that it was shown on National television at 2pm in the afternoon.

As Lawrence left the studio he muttered 'Wanker.'

'What did he say?' Asked Powell.

Even though Powell did not object to participants using foul language on his show. He would not tolerate being on the receiving end of it. 'What did say?' He repeated.

It was Nicola that rescued a situation that could have turned ugly. 'He said wanted to thank yer.' She said.

A grin spread across Powell's face, he looked like a Cheshire cat, as he said 'Marshall will be on the judging panel for the televised stages. We will not warn him about the man's condition, we will say nothing and leave it to Marshall to speak with him, when the bloke starts swearing at him it will be hilarious. I can't wait.'

Lewis Marshall was the third judge on The Factor. Powell disliked him but due to his contacts in the media, he employed him on the judging panel.

Chlamydia

The door opened and in stepped a man dressed from top to toe in women's clothing, on his head he was wearing a mousy coloured shoulder length wig, on his face was full make-up, but despite the fact that the time was a just little bit after midday the five o'clock shadow beneath it was still visible. The dress he wore was floral and the shoes had four inch stiletto heels. He was six feet five inches tall in his bare feet and much broader than average across the shoulders. He looked like a giant.

Mellissa greeted him in her usual pleasant way with. 'Come in and tell us a little bit about yourself.'

'Well Darling, you see the problem is I am a woman trapped in a man's body and that is what's been stopping me from making a career in show business. I could be the new Madonna or Cher if I was just given the chance to prove myself, then I would be able to afford an operation to release me from this hell that I am trapped in. You see they won't give me the operation on the National Health Service and so I shall have to pay for it myself.'

As she looked at the clipboard that she had in front of her Mellissa replied. 'So I see on my notes you are a poet and what are you going to recite for us today Chlamydia? ....Chlamydia?'

'Yes darling it's kind of novel isn't it? My parents named me Reginald Albert Robinson. That just has to be the dullest name ever, so I changed it by deed poll to Chlamydia.'

'Chlamydia Robinson?'

'No darling, just Chlamydia, having a forename and a family name is so last year, in fact it's not even last year, it's last century.'

'So Chlamydia are you going to recite a poem for us today?'

'Yes Darling, I am going to perform for you a beautiful little poem that I wrote myself, it's called "Man's a bitch" You will love it darling.'

Oh why would anyone want to be a man?
If you can't tell me, then who can?
Better to be a Lady full of grace
With a curvaceous body and a pretty face
When I was an egg Mother Nature was silly
She placed on my person a tiny little Willy
I begged the N.H.S to give an op
Oh please dear doctor give it a chop
Men burp and sneeze and pick their nose
And why he scratches so much? Heaven knows
A man is vulgar from the start
He raises his leg to let off a fart

Powell cut in, he did not need to hear anymore.

Waving his hand in the air he declared. 'Ok that's enough, you have proved yourself, and you are on the show.'

Chlamydia was ecstatic, he looked deep into Powell's eyes and began to approach him as he said. 'Oh Darling thank you, thank you so much, I could kiss you, I could kiss you all over.'

Powell stood up sharply as he said. 'That will not be necessary speak to my team, they will give you the relevant details.'

'Oh Darling, can I just say one thing?'

'Yes but say it to the camera.'

Chlamydia looked into the camera, he was ecstatic as he said. 'All I ever wanted to do since I was a little girl was to perform. I always knew I was set for stardom. I have known from the very beginning that my place was onstage in front of my adoring fans, and you are giving me the chance to do that. I love you, I love so very much.' As Chlamydia was speaking tears began to roll down his cheeks and his make-up was running.

Nobody spoke, the camera had zoomed in on him.

The camera's would not normally be there at this stage of the auditions, but as Powell was present, the cameras were there also ready to capture any moment that they may be able to give air time too and this was gold, a giant of a man dressed in woman's clothing sobbing as he thanked the man himself for giving him this opportunity.

Then suddenly he completely broke down, he was sobbing his heart out uncontrollably, and he could no longer speak. What a bonus this was everybody on The Factor team knew this was a moment that they could use over and over in the trailers.

Mellissa and Nicola were not going to let this moment pass, here was their opportunity to show the world how kind and caring that they really are.

Mellissa jumped from her chair and put a caring hand on his shoulder as she simultaneously said. 'That is what we are here for, to make dreams come true, it's why Mister Powell started The Factor.'

Nicola was rubbing her hand up and down Chlamydia's back as he was sobbing. 'Thank you, thank you so much.'

Chlamydia carried on sobbing and thanking everyone as he was being led from the studio.

When he was out Powell looked at Jason the head camera man and asked. 'Did you get that?'

Jason was feeling quite pleased with himself as he answered. 'It's all in the can Baby. You know you can always count on me.'

'Don't call me Baby. Don't anyone ever dare call me Baby?' Was Powell's stern reply. He then said. 'That is not what I'm really looking for, we have over done it with the sympathy pitch, but he is in, that will make good telly. Get me as much background information on him as you can. I want you to find out about his passed relationships, has he ever been married? Is he gay? Has he ever been in trouble with the police? Has he got a family? If so find out as much as you can about them. How do they feel about him wanting to spend the rest of his life dressed as a woman? If we get the story right this one could pull in the viewers. Give his details to Burke and Hare. I have got a good feeling about this one

Chris the Greek

Next through the door came a group of four, three men and one woman, two of the men were dressed from top to toe as police officers.

Powell liked the look of them, if ever there was a quartet of odd looking people here they were.

The first one through the door was a tall thin grey haired man in his late forties, he was smartly dressed in a grey two piece suit and tie. He was followed by a short stocky woman, she was as broad as she was tall and she had short spiky sticking up hair and was also dressed in a grey two piece suit and tie. They were followed by two men with blank "Where am I?" Expressions on their faces, and were scruffily dressed in police uniforms. If you saw them you would have thought Tweedle Dee and Tweedle Dum. Powell liked the look of them, whatever these misfits did for an act, they would certainly be on the first televised show and get their ten minutes of fame.

The tall thin one walked over to where Powell was sitting and opened what looked like a credit card holder, as he held it twelve inches from his face, he said 'Detective inspector Roger Ainsdale Mister Powell. Is there anywhere we can have a quiet chat?'

Powell, liked that, he smiled as he said. 'I understand your gimmick and you have my nod of approvable. Now tell me what do you do for an act?'

'No you don't understand Mister Powell. My Name is Detective Inspector Ainsdale and this is Detective Inspector Shanklin, we are conducting a murder enquiry and would like to have a word with you. I will ask you one more time. Do you have anywhere that we can go for a quiet chat? Or would you prefer to accompany us to the police station?'

You could have heard a pin drop, Powell's chin hit the floor, he took a few seconds to compose himself, and he swallowed hard, then said. 'Come with me, I have a courtesy room through here.'

Ainsdale and Shanklin followed Powell through the door into the plush courtesy room, they closed the door behind them. Tweedle Dum and Tweedle Dee stood guard outside and prevented Jason from going in.

'Let me in you jumped up fucking Nazi's.' Screamed Jason as he was waving his arms protesting.

'If you say one more word you will be arrested for obstructing the police in their line of duty, so sit down and behave yourself.' Said Tweedle Dee.

Inside the courtesy room Powell was shown a 5x4 inch photograph of Christopher Charles Farrington. A.K.A "Chris the Greek." He was not Greek but he introduced himself to everyone he met as Chris the Greek, he felt the name had a certain kind of ring to it.

As Powell was looking at the photograph he was informed that Farrington's dead body had been found on Sunday morning in his flat in South London.

'What has this got to do with me? I know nothing about this man and I have never seen or heard of him before.' Said Powell.

He was then shown a photograph of himself posing with a tall leggy blonde woman on his left arm and Chris the Greek standing to his right.

'Can you explain this?' Ainsdale asked.

'No I can't, but I will say that I get photo bombed everywhere I go.' Answered Powell defensively.

It was true there are thousands of people like Chris the Greek that love to have their photograph taken with anyone that is a household name. With or without their consent. The walls of the deceased man's living room were plastered with framed photographs of himself and some of the biggest names in show business.

Therefore Powell's explanation was believable.

On this occasion whilst Powell was publicly posing for a pic for a glossy magazine the Greek had given his mobile phone to someone to take the pic that he was now looking at as he shook his head from side to side.

'He was killed by a blow to the head with a blunt instrument.' Said Ainsdale. 'We are not sure of the exact date or time of his death, two of our officers went to his home to arrest him last week for breaking his condition of bail by failing to report to the police station. When they entered the flat they found his decomposing body.

He was under investigation for fraud.'

'But what has this got to do with me?' Asked Powell.
'We have had eleven separate complaints from people
claiming to have been conned by him and the common
denominator is that they have all appeared on your show.'
Ainsdale then explained to Powell that. 'The man in
question was a very clever fraudster without any morals
whatsoever. Despite the numerous complaints that we
have received about him, we have not yet managed to get
enough evidence for the C.P.S to prosecute. Even though
we do not know the exact time and date of his death, the
autopsy report indicates that he was killed approximately
21days prior to our officers finding him.'
Powell thought for a second then said. 'I was not in the
country then, last month I was on-board my private yacht
in the Caribbean.'
'We know that.' Replied Ainsdale. 'You are not a suspect
Mister Powell, but we need to investigate the connection
between his murder and the people that have appeared on
your show that he has conned. I have a list of people here
and I would appreciate your co-operation in giving me as
much information on them as you can.'
Powell assured them that he would help them in any way
he that he possibly could and that they would receive the
fullest co-operation from himself and the employees of
Power-Man Productions.

Trevor the Traffic Warden

A strange looking man with a head that did not seem to match his body entered the studio.

He was a certainty to make it to the live show.

He was what Powell was looking for.

Mellissa smiled at him and said. 'Can you tell us a little bit about yourself and what you are going to do for us today?'

'My name is Trevor and I am Forty two years of age and I am a civil enforcement officer.'

'Does that mean you give out parking tickets?' Powell Asked.

'Yes Sir, I have earned my place in society by serving Queen and country.' Trevor proudly replied.

'And what are you going to do for us today?'

'I am going to swallow six hard boiled eggs.'

Trevor then opened the egg box he was holding and produced an egg still in its shell and swallowed it whole.

He then produced another then another, until he had swallowed six hard boiled eggs all of which were still in their shells.

The studio was silent, the crew were dumbstruck by the sight that they had just witnessed.

Trevor broke the silence by holding out his arms by his side and proudly declaring. 'Daaa Laaaar.'

'What will happen to the eggs now? Are you going to regurgitate them?' Powell asked.

'No I will just wait for Mother Nature to take its course.'

'Have you done this before?'

Trevor liked the attention he was getting his face was beaming as he replied. 'No I wanted this to be the first time I did it to really impress you.'

Everybody was puzzled. It was Mellissa that asked the question that was on everyone's mind. 'Can the body process eggs when they are boiled and swallowed whole whilst they are still in their shell?'

Nobody knew the answer, so everybody agreed that Trevor should immediately take himself to the local hospital accident and emergency department.

Trevor did relish the thought of going to the hospital A&E department with a medical problem that he had brought upon himself.

 Only six months previously an irate driver that had caught him in the act of placing a parking fine on his car windscreen, pointed his finger at the machine he used to print the tickets with and shouted. "You can stick that thing up your arse." When Trevor got home he thought he would give it a try, he had never had a sexual partner, apart from an indiscretion with a sheep when he was in his twenty's. (See the novel Conscience). So he was forever trying to think up new ways of pleasuring himself. All was well until the muscles in his anal passage contracted and the machine became wedged between his buttocks.

He cried out in pain and his elderly mother that he lived with on entering his bedroom, scolded him before calling for an ambulance. "When will you stop doing these perverted things? We had to move home and change our family name and get new identities after you shamed us when you got convicted of bestiality. You disgusting creature."

Now Trevor was having to go back to the same A&E department, where the nurse in charge has also scolded him six months previously.

Bizarre

The next person to enter the studio was a rather large woman. She did not wait to be asked any question.
'My names Samantha I am sixty four years old and I am a Burlesque dancer.'
The lady that stood before them was obese and she was definitely no oil painting. Her bleached blond hair was full of split ends and her black roots were showing through.
She had over done it with her make-up, it looked like it had been put on with a bricklayers trowel and her bright red lipstick was on her teeth.
The only way I could describe her clothing would be to say that she had no dress sense whatsoever.
Therefore the image of Samantha gyrating whilst simultaneously taking her clothes off was not something that The Factor crew relished.
Despite that she was instructed to go ahead.
She started to hum some kind of a tune whilst she without any rhythm whatsoever shook her body and removed her clothes. When her skirt came off she revealed a tiny black thong that would not even fit a Hamster, with most of it disappearing inside her extremely large buttocks.
When she took her corset off the rolls of fat dropped and covered her pelvis. Whilst her considerably large breasts dropped to her waistline as she attempted to twirl the

crimson coloured tassels attached to her nipples by shaking her body in a circular motion.

Some of the crew sniggered, while others shook their heads in disbelief.

Powell did not need to see anymore. 'That will be enough for now, give the crew your full details and I will see you on the show.'

Samantha picked up her clothes, satisfied that she had given a notable performance and very happily left the studio.

The studio doors opened and Nicola was followed in by Tamara. She had no less than twenty eight facial piercings, in fact her face was barely visible. Her backcombed hair was way passed her shoulders and was extremely untidy. She wore an old pair of jeans that were torn and looked like they needed a wash and a black T-shirt with the motif.

Sisters are doing for themselves

Powell immediately took an interest in her, he spoke first. 'Hello, tell me your name and why you think you have got what it takes to make it in the entertainment industry.'

'My name is Tamara and I am going to sing.'

Powell rolled his eyes and looked upwards as he said. 'You haven't answered my question. What is it that you think you have to make a career in show business?'

'I dunno what you mean.' Tamara replied.

Mellissa then said. 'What Mister Powell is asking you is. What made you take up singing? And do think you have what it takes to make it?'

'Make what?'

'A career in show business.'

'Oh I see what you mean. Yeh I have.'

'So why did you take up singing?' Asked Mellissa.

'Well what happened was I was living with this bloke you see, and well I suspected that he was mucking about with someone else, so I set a trap. I told him I was going away for the weekend to visit my sick auntie. That was a lie, I mean don't even have an auntie let alone a sick one. But I had to find out what was going on. You know how it is don't you Mellissa? So what I did was I stayed out till three in the morning, then I sneaked in and I saw them. They were fast asleep, in my bed, stark bollock naked. I said you cunt and I picked up one of the cider bottles off of the floor and I threw it at him. Let's be fair you'd do the same wouldn't yer? And do you know he said?'

The dumbstruck Mellissa just shook her head.

'He jumped out of bed and he said. "Darling it's alright, I can explain." I said explain this. Then I picked up another bottle and smashed it over his fucking head. Be fair Mellissa. What would you have done?'

Mellissa was terrified she just shook her head as she answered. 'I don't know.'

Tamara carried on. 'Well he just fell on the floor holding his head, then he got up and said. "It's not what it looks like." I said well what does it look like? It don't look like a fucking Teddy Bears picnic. Then I smacked him in the gob. What got me was she was an absolute minger. Her tattoos weren't even spelt right. My bloke was mucking about with an old slapper like that. When he had a classy bird like me. So I thought that's it, I am gonna to make summink of my life. I'm gonna be a singer.

Powell liked this girl, she had what he would describe as character. 'You seem to have an awful lot of piercings, how many do you have in total?' He asked.

'Well I've got these ones on my face and about twenty on my body.' As she spoke Tamara lifted up her top to reveal piercings all over her stomach and through her breasts. 'And I've got five down there through my…..'

Mellissa cut in. 'That's nice would you like to sing for us now?'

Tamara screeched for two minutes, it was painful, it was like somebody attacking your eardrums with a pneumatic drill. Powell help up his hand for her to stop, then he said. 'I think you're marvellous you are on the show.' He then looked at Mellissa and asked. So what do you think?'

Mellissa was stunned, she simply answered. 'Yes.'

Tamara was elated as she left the studio she said to Mellissa and Powell. 'I love you two, you're the best.'

Next through the studio doors came Angela.

Powell was instantly disinterested, when Mellissa asked her about herself, her answer was. 'My name is Angela I am thirty three years old and I am currently studying music. Today I would like to sing for you a little number that I have wrote myself.'

As soon as she began Powell decided that he was going to dismiss her. Angela could sing there was no doubting that. She was also well presented and reasonably attractive. But there was nothing about her that he felt would grab the viewers. He could not understand why the crew had allowed her into the studio today. Today was for the bizarre. A crew member walked over to Powell and placed a sheet of paper in front of him. His eyes lit up.

When Angela finished singing Powell said. 'That was very good you have definitely got The Factor. In fact you have the very talent that I am looking for.'

'Thank you.'

'I see that you have been in a few adult movies. Would you like to tell me about those?'

'That was ten years ago, I was out of work and living on my own, I could not afford to pay the bills, somebody suggested that if I starred in those films I would make lots of money, at the time it seemed like the best thing to do. I regret it now, I am trying to put that behind me and concentrate on my music career.'

Powell was liking this girl now, he was liking her a lot.

A big friendly smile spread across his face as he said. 'Angela you can certainly put those films behind you now. The Factor is a family show and pornography would be totally unacceptable. Let me kick start your music career for you now, by informing you that you are on the show.'

Angela was elated she could not stop thanking Powell. When she exited the studio he turned to the crew and said. 'I want to see copies of those films. She will appear on the first audition and we will vote her through to the second round. Then I want it leaked to the press that a porn star is now a contestant on The Factor. Of course we never knew anything about it. Give her details to Burke and Hare they can start working on this one now.'

Doing Bird?

Powell was feeling quite pleased with himself, the misfits had not disappointed him they were as usual in abundance. He was also satisfied that he had the right amount of people with sufficient talent and background stories to make the show a success.

Then suddenly the studio door opened and George Answell appeared bursting straight into a song. He did this with such an air of confidence that every single member of the twelve strong crew present could see that he was a real showman. His voice was pitch perfect and he performed as he sang like a seasoned professional.

As everybody in the studio looked on and listened appreciatively they were feeling like they had finally discovered genuine talent.

But not Powell, this angered him, he recognized this man as someone he had previously dismissed and he had not authorized a second audition. As the song finished he bellowed. 'Who offered you a call back?'

Answell humbly replied. 'Mister Powell, I didn't tell you the truth when I came here before because I was afraid that if you knew about my previous, you would not have put me on the show.'

Powell now leapt up from his chair with his arms outstretched and his palms wide open as he repeated. 'Who offered you a call back?'

'Well … I've been doing bird?'

'Doing bird?'

'Yes Mister Powell four years, four years in the Ville,'

'The Vile?'

'Yes Mister Powell Pentonville Nick, manslaughter, but it weren't my fault, I was in a boozer and some geezer picked a fight with me and well how was I supposed to know he heart a heart condition?'

Here we have a story, suddenly Powell became interested.

'Are you telling me you killed a man?'

'Yes but I didn't mean to. It was an accident. I served my time. Now I can't get a job or nothing.'

'So what did you do before that? What did you do before you killed that man?'

'I did a bit of door work and a bit of debt collecting?'

'So why can't you go back to that?'

'Too many people know don't they, I mean they don't mind a bit of G.B.H. That's acceptable, it keeps the punters in order, and it goes to show you won't take no nonsense, but murder?'

'Murder? Correct me if I am wrong. But I thought you said manslaughter.'

'Manslaughter, murder, same thing ain't it? The geezers dead and I've done the bird. At the time it was all over the news, now no one wants to touch me.'

Powell was mocking him as he asked. 'So answer this little question. If I don't put you on the show, what will you do? Kill me?'

'I don't want to kill anyone Mister Powell. If I don't get a break I will have to live on benefits, what I am saying Mister Powell is I don't want to live on benefits.'

'Just hold on a minute.' Powell said as he was now walking around in a circle thinking of a way that he could use this man's tale. As he spoke he was waving his finger. 'That's not right, that won't sell, if you can't make it as a rock star you will go back to a life of crime.'

'I won't, that's the point. I have never been a criminal.'

'Now listen to me.' Powell said assertively. 'You are going to say that some of your mates that you met in prison have offered you a job, it's not legal but highly lucrative and you might have to hurt a few people and you are tempted to take it, so this is your last chance, your only hope of making something of your life and I am going to give it to you.'

'No, no no that is not true, I'm just looking for work. There is no way I'm going to hurt anyone.'

This irritated Powell, he wasn't use to people saying no to him, but he allowed Answell to have that one as he felt that he could take advantage of his story.

Powell looked him in the eye and said. 'Now listen to me, do you want to live on benefits?'

'No, no not at all Mister Powell. All I want to do is earn an honest living.'

'So let us get this straight, you cannot get a job because you have a criminal record, not just any old criminal record, you killed a man and if I don't give you a break, you are going to spend your life living off of benefits in a tiny little flat. This is your last chance to be someone. To get yourself a life. You need me Georgie boy.'

'Yes I do Trenton.'

'Mister Powell to you. I never gave you permission to address me by my Christian name.'

Powell like to be called Trenton when the show was on air by everyone. It showed the viewing public, what a friendly down to earth chap he was, but behind the scenes he insisted on being called "Mister" or "Sir."

'Sorry! Yes Mister Powell.' Replied Answell humbly. Satisfied that he was now totally in control Powell disclosed the strategy he would adopt for him. 'Now this is what we are going to do, we will remind everyone that you are a killer, but I will bring you back from a life of crime and give you the chance to go straight.'

Answell protested meekly. 'But I have never been a bad violent person, it really was an accident.'

Powell's voice was harsher and the volume increased a touch. 'You killed a man in a bar-room brawl and I am going to give you the chance to repent and make a career for yourself. Do you want that or do you want to just leave here now and?' Powell paused for a few seconds then waved his hand in a dismissive way as he turned his back and said. 'Just forget it, go on, go away.'

'No, no please I need this chance Mister Powell, I really don't have any options, I am begging you, and I won't let you down.'

Satisfied that he had the man exactly where he wanted him and that he would say and do whatever he was told.

Powell smirked as he said. 'Okay you do and say what I

tell you and I will give you a career. We will be in touch, you can go now.'

As George Answell was leaving Powell turned to Mellissa and said. 'I think we can really make something of this, we have never had a murderer on the show before. Get a camera crew sent over to his home, I want as much background information on him as we can get. Does he have a family? If he has I want my team to find out as much as they can about them. Tell them to dig as deep as they need too. Has he been in trouble before? If he has what was it? What was he like at school? Was he a good kid or a bad kid? And most important I want to find the victim's family, I want to know everything about the man he killed. What did he do for a living? Did he have any children? Has he left behind a grieving widow forced to bring up young children on her own? Everybody has a family, I want photographs of the victim's family holding a photograph of their loved one that Answell killed. Ask them how they feel about his killer being allowed to walk the streets, whilst their loved one is lying dead? How do they feel about the man that took his life appearing on national television? Does it sicken them that the man who murdered their loved one is on his way to a successful career? We will dig deep and dig dirty. If we can get this one right the interest will be enormous.'

Saint Tropez

It was now Thursday afternoon. The clock on the wall showed the time was 4.35 and Powell knew that he had enough hopefuls to make his show.

There were twelve talented ones with interesting tales to tell and an abundance of freaks, screamers and sobers with no talent whatsoever to give him and his sadistic audience something to mock.

He puffed out his chest leant back in his chair and declared. 'That is it, I have had enough. We can wrap it up now. And I want some of you to get your arses over to the hotel.'

Mellissa looked at her watch and the notes that she had on the table in front of her then said. 'But Mister Powell there are still a lot of people waiting to see you, they have been here all day, in fact some of them have been waiting to see you since Monday.'

Not in the least bit interested about the hoard of people gathered in the large hall that he called a green room Powell uncaringly replied. 'They can come back another day if I need them; I have had enough for now and you have got a plane to catch.'

Mellissa looked puzzled. 'An aeroplane.'

'Yes an aeroplane, we talked about it on Monday remember you're going to Saint Tropez for the weekend and your weekend starts now.'

Mellissa shook her head and said pleadingly 'But Mister Powell it is Joseph's Mum's 60th birthday today and we are taking her out to dinner this evening.'

'Joseph can take his mum out to dinner. But not you. You will be going out to dinner in Saint Tropez with Abdikarim Dalmar, it has all been arranged. There's no need for you to pack, everything you need has been sorted and will be in the boot of the car taking you to the airport.'

'But Mister Powell I really don't think I should go.'

The volume of Powell's voice rose and his tone became harsh as he retorted. 'I will tell you what you should do. You will go to Saint Tropez with a premiership footballer for the weekend, you will be seen on his arm everywhere you go, you will wear the garments that have been chosen for you, you will do it with a smile on your face and you will get the maximum amount of publicity that you possibly can.'

Mellissa really did not want to be going anywhere with a man that she had never met, or had any communication with whatsoever.

She tried to reason with Powell. 'I don't think me going away for a weekend with a footballer will help the show. What if we do a story about how Joseph and I are planning on getting married next year and how we spend most of our free time helping abandoned animals? I think the newspapers and their readers would like that. It would be good publicity for The Factor and ....'

Powell did not let her finish, she had pushed his patience as far as he would allow. Despite the fact that she was sat right beside Powell his bellow could be heard from 100 yards away. 'I have already told you if I wanted somebody to think I would not have employed you. Now you have two choices. You rather do as I say and go to Saint Tropez for the weekend, or you go home and never work for Power-Man productions ever again. The choice is yours. What are you going to do?'

'I will do what you say Mister Powell but I am worried about Joseph, I had better call him and let him know what I am doing.' As she spoke Mellissa stood up and took her mobile phone from her handbag.

Powell snatched it from her. Then pointing to the door he replied assertively. 'There is no need to call him, you can speak to him when you get back. The paparazzi will be waiting in Saint Tropez for you, the next time I see your cute little arse it had better be in the tabloids. Go now there's a car waiting for you. I have got as a busy weekend lined up myself.' As he finished speaking Powell slapped Mellissa hard on the buttocks.

With tears in her eyes and a lump in her throat Mellissa made her way towards the limousine that would be taking her to the airport.

You're The Man

They were expecting to receive a telephone call, or an E-mail, or maybe a letter. So they were totally taken by surprise when the two people one male and one female both around thirty years of age came knocking on their door and explained that they were from Power-Man Productions.

They were even more surprised and absolutely delighted when they were informed that "Mister Trenton Powell was so impressed with your performance at the audition that not only have you been guaranteed a place on the live show, he has also sent us to take you to a five star hotel, where you will staying free of charge and you will receive a full make-over and will be fully trained in how to perform in front of the camera and you will also have your own voice coach."

This was a dream come true for the twins.

Excitedly they began to pack and as Mary-Anne was doing so, the woman from Power-Man Productions was informing her that "The next few weeks would be the most exciting that you have ever had in your life, it will be like a giant rollercoaster ride that will never want to stop."

Charlotte was her name although she introduced herself as "Lottie" which was how she preferred to be addressed. Lottie was slim with shoulder length auburn coloured hair and despite being casually dressed in a pair of light blue denim jeans and a navy blue crew necked jumper, she looked very presentable and had an extremely likeable manner about her.

In the next room Sebastian was fidgeting with excitement as he stood with his feet together bouncing up and down on the spot but without actually leaving the ground. Lottie's colleague Graham who was just five feet seven inches tall but of stocky build with a round face and a head that shown no sign of ever having hair was keeping Sebastian amused and keeping the enthusiasm up by saying. 'You're going to be the man. Who are you going to be?'

To which Sebastian answered. 'I'm going to be the man.'

'Who are you?'

'I'm the man.'

Mary-Anne had packed everything that she felt they would need for the next couple of weeks, which was pretty much all of their clothing and all of the toiletries they owned. The twins were then lead to the car as they excitedly set off for an adventure that would change their lives forever.

How Fortunate Are You?

It was 4.30 pm on Sunday afternoon and there they were
in the main hall of a thirty seven bedroom hotel in Dorset.
Seven months had passed since the hotel had officially
closed, the owners William and Irene Peterson were both
in their seventies and due too ill health were desperately
trying to sell, all of their capital was tied up in the hotel
and they so much wanted to retire.
 But despite dropping the price to almost 70% of the
original asking price, they could still not find a buyer.
Therefore they welcomed Power-Man Productions that
saw their hotel as an ideal location to nurture the
participants for the forthcoming series of The Factor.
Even though Powell was only paying a nominal amount
for the sole use of the entire building, the Peterson's felt
that the exposure the hotel would receive from this project
may attract a buyer.
The atmosphere inside the hall was electrifying, every
single person chosen to be there was as excited as a five
year old child on Christmas Eve.
There was a camera crew, hair-stylists, beauticians and no
less than seven additional crew members whose sole
purpose was to keep the excitement alive.
Special attention was paid to Sebastian who remained
constantly by the side of his sister Mary-Anne, he would
not let go of her hand and he no longer felt as enthusiastic
as he had before, he now seemed apprehensive, the energy
and excitement within the room made him nervous he kept
asking the same question. "When are we going home?"

Sebastian had two interests in life his sister Mary-Anne and trains. He was totally fascinated with trains. And so a crew member was instructed to go to the shops and purchase the biggest and the best train set that he could possibly find for Sebastian.

On a big screen footage was being shown of previous Factor winners. Every two minutes up came the words "This could be you." The sound from the speakers that had been placed in every corner of the hall was louder than it needed to be.

Suddenly the sound was muted and a spotlight was focused on the entrance to the hall, then in walked the main man himself, the crew as they had been instructed to do so, stood up and applauded and cheered enthusiastically, every single person in the hall followed suit and even though there were only thirty eight people present the noise was deafening causing Sebastian to cover his ears.

Powell smirked then gestured for every person present to stop applauding and take a seat. It was now time for him to make his welcome speech, he had not done this before, it was usual for him to leave this stage of the preparation of The Factor series to his team.

But due to their incompetence the show had taken a serious nosedive and he now felt that only he and he alone, could put The Factor back on top.

There was silence for a few seconds as Powell slowly looked around the room being sure to catch the eye of every person present.

He relished this moment he felt like Jesus preaching to his thousands of followers as he said. 'Welcome to what for the next eight weeks will be your home and you don't need me to tell you how fortunate you are to be here in my presence.'

The Power-Man crew felt positively nauseous, they resented their arrogant self-indulgent boss, they wanted to reach for the sick bucket to fill with vomit and tip it all over the conceited bastards head.

But they didn't, they applauded and everybody inside the hall followed suit.

He continued. 'The reason that you have been chosen to be here is because you have got what it takes to go the whole way, to make it through to the final stages of The Factor. Some of you will be given major recording contracts, and one of the lucky acts among you will appearing at The London Palladium on The Royal Variety Show.' Again there was a pause and again more applause.

'It will not be easy, nobody ever said that it would be easy, but it will be fun, it will be an experience that the majority of people would give their right arm for. I am the man that can make all of your dreams come true. And if you listen to my advice your dreams will come true. We will now set about getting you ready for the first programme of the new series.'

Powell then turned to exit the room, as he did so all of the person's present stood up and applauded.

Lottie had been assigned to Mary-Anne. It were her job to prepare her for the forthcoming series.

The twins were sitting in the corner holding hands.

Lottie approached them, she noticed that Mary-Anne was comforting her brother.

When she was in earshot, she heard her say. 'Everything will be fine Sebastian, we are going to have so much fun together.'

Lottie gave her a big friendly smile as she said. 'I will take you to wardrobe now, we have some outfits for you to try on, and a beautician is waiting to give you a full make-over for the publicity shots.'

The twins stood up and still holding hands began to follow her. Lottie felt uneasy, this was awkward, as she had been instructed to bring the girl to wardrobe without her brother. As she was contemplating what to do, like a knight in shining armour Graham came to the rescue.

As he walked in holding a large box and stretching his hands out towards Sebastian he happily announced.

'Power-Man Productions with the compliments of Mister Trenton Powell have a gift for you.'

Sebastian's eyes lit up as he gazed at the gift and stated. 'That is The Flying Scotsman 00 gauge electric train set. Do you know that The Flying Scotsman was first built in 1862? It is powered by steam and runs from London to Edinburgh. And The Flying Scotsman was the first ever train to........'

Graham cut in before he could say anymore and thrusting the box into his chest, forcing Sebastian to let go of his sisters hand and take the gift he said. 'Yes and it is my honour to present you with this extraordinary gift. We have a spare conference room set aside for you and me to assemble this whole set.'

As pleased as anyone could have ever been Sebastian asked. 'Can we build a lay-out with buildings and fields and farmyard animal's?'

Graham did not know what a lay-out was, he had never heard the term lay-out before, and so he answered. 'Yes of course we can, come on let us go and do it now.'

And so the two of them happily made their way into the room that had a wooden plaque on the door marked conference room two.

Mary-Anne was now feeling much happier than she had felt in a long while. Sebastian does not normally mix well with other people and he only leaves her side when one of them is going to the bathroom.

However Graham and the entire crew of Power-Man Productions seem to have an understanding of his condition. She was delighted that Sebastian had instantly made good friends with Graham.

As she followed Lottie to wardrobe she was completely satisfied that her twin was happy and being cared for.

Mary-Anne was not materialistic, she could not afford to be, even though she was always well presented, she possessed very few items of clothing and so when Lottie escorted her into the room that had a sheet of A4 sized paper stuck onto the door with Blu Tack, with the words Mary-Anne Wardrobe written on it. The only thing she could say was "Wow."

As Mary-Anne was looking in awe at all of the elaborate outfits Lottie explained that "This room and all of the costumes inside have been set aside solely for you."

Again Mary-Anne replied "Wow."

Broken Hearts and Busted Phones

Joseph was sitting there feeling numb as he stared at the
newspaper placed on the coffee table in front of him.
The headlines on the front page were accompanied by a
photograph of the woman he loved on a beach with sea
water just passed her ankles as she was paddling whilst
wearing nothing but a tiny thong, her breasts had a white
line over them where the nipples would be. Across them
was the word **"Censored"** The headlines read:
 "Who is T.Vs Golden Girl Frolicking With?"
The column at the side went on to explain that Mellissa
Parker had been spotted by photographers whilst on
holiday in Saint Tropez with her new lover.
Then on the bottom of the front page were the words
"Turn to pages three, four, five and six to see more
revealing pictures and discover who the mystery
premiership footballer is."
Joseph did not need to turn to pages three, four, five and
six again he had just spent the past three hours totally
distraught whilst looking at the photographs of the most
important person in his life, frolicking on the beach with
the man that the newspapers had described as
"The bad boy of football"
The inner pages of the tabloid papers were not censored.
Mellissa's boobs and buttocks were exposed for everyone

to see. Joseph was not bothered by them. It was pictures of Mellissa and the footballer rubbing sun protection cream over each-others near naked bodies that upset him.

The story that accompanied the pictures made him feel sick to the bottom of his gut.

"Mellissa Parker the golden girl of television has dumped her fiancé Joseph and has begun a steamy affair with footballs bad boy Abdikarim Dalmar.

It was rumoured that she was going to quit showbiz and the jet set lifestyle to marry her love struck boyfriend. However a source close to the Power-Man Production company has revealed that, the affair has come as no surprise to them."

The first time that Joseph and Mellissa had met was whilst he was helping out in his spare time as a volunteer at a rescue centre for abandoned dogs.

An open day had been organised to raise awareness of the project and to also raise much needed funds, as the home received no government funding, it relied solely on charitable donations.

The project was well supported by the local radio and the local press.

Mellissa lived local, and was quite a celebrity in the area in which she lived, the previous year she was invited to turn on the Christmas lights in the town centre. The prestigious 1400 seater theatre in the town centre had cast her as the leading lady in the annual pantomime.

She was also a real animal lover, and so when she heard about the project she volunteered to go along for the day and help out at the centre.

If you do not believe in love at first sight believe it now, because that is exactly what it was when the eyes of Mellissa and Joseph met for the first time.

They could no longer hear the sound of barking dogs, or the people applauding approvingly as Mellissa entered the canine sanctuary, they could not see the flash from the camera's as the photographers were hastily snapping away. The only sight they saw for that few precious seconds was the pure beauty of each other.

That was three years ago and since the day that they first met they had become totally devoted to each other, spending every spare moment they had together and planning their future, even choosing names for the children they were planning to have.

But now it was all over. Mellissa never told him it was over. She had never mentioned the other guy. Joseph had not even received a text from her.

"Going away on business for a few days. Keep the bed warm for me. P.S I Love you lots and lots x x x x x."

Would have been the message he would have expected to receive from her, if she would not be returning home for a few days, but she had told him nothing.

He had tried to call her on her mobile phone several times since she had not returned home from work on Thursday evening. But every time he called the call was diverted directly to her voicemail and each time he left a message. Joseph grew concerned, he was beside himself with worry. On the few occasions when they had spent time apart they constantly called and texted each other.

He contacted a colleague of Mellissa's at Power-Man Productions to see if she knew of her whereabouts, the answer he received was "She never said anything about her plans for the weekend to me."

Joseph phoned every single one of Mellissa's friends that he knew the number of, but not one of them had any idea of where she might be.

He then called the local hospitals and the police, he reported her as a missing person. The police advised him to "Sit by the phone and we will contact you as soon as we have any information regarding her whereabouts."

The police never called, nobody called.

It was different this morning, his telephone had been ringing constantly, it seemed as if every friend, family member and acquaintance had called, with the opening line. "Have you seen today's newspapers?"

The callers then went on to tell Joseph "I am so sorry." Which was followed by the classic cliché "She doesn't deserve you, you can do so much better for yourself, you are better off without her."

Although Joseph appreciated their support, he did not want sympathy, he certainly did not want to be told that he is better off without the woman he loves more than life itself. He replied with a polite "Thank you" then immediately cut the caller off each time.

The hardest call to take came from his mother. "I knew this would happen one day, any girl that takes her clothes off and runs around stark naked in front of all those people for the whole world to see on television is no good."

The call from his mother reduced Joseph to floods of tears.

But it was the call made by a journalist from a national newspaper that had infuriated, the otherwise passive Joseph and caused him to react in a manner that was far removed from his usual behaviour. "Hello Joseph Reynolds, I am from news national and I would like to ask you if you were aware of your fiancée Mellissa Parker's affair with the footballer Abdikarim Dalmar?"

Joseph responded by screaming "Fuck off you parasite" into the receiver before he bashed it repeatedly on the table until it was totally broken beyond repair.

He then picked up his mobile and threw in to the floor and stamped on it continuously until it was smashed to pieces. Joseph had never committed any act of vandalism before but the endless stream of phone calls he had received that morning, mostly sympathetic from genuine friends and others from people calling to gloat had driven to react in a manner that was totally out of his usual character.

They never knew the real Mellissa. They never knew the loving caring girl that he had the joy of sharing a home and his life with. But now here they were casting judgement on her and telling him what a fool he was to have fallen for her in the first place.

In The News

"The newspaper you asked for has arrived Mister Powell."
There were only two occasions when Powell would insist
on being addressed by his Christian name by any person
that he considered to be beneath him. (Which was pretty
much everybody) One of those was for the benefit of the
television camera and the other was just after he had
shagged the person that was speaking to him.
So when the stunningly attractive twenty two year old
with long blonde hair that went almost half way down her
back, wearing nothing but a white fluffy towel that she
had taken from the bathroom to wrap around herself when
she answered the door to the bellboy in order to prevent
him from catching an eyeful of her naked flesh, walked
towards the hotel bed that he was sat upright in, and
addressed him as "Mister Powell" as she held out the
tabloid newspaper for him, he corrected her with.
'Trenton. Call me Trenton, there is no need to be formal.'
A broad smile spread across his face when he saw the
headlines, then turned to pages three, four, five and six,
this was exactly what he was wanting. This was exactly
what he had planned to orchestrate.
They were back in the national tabloid papers. Surely now
the gossip magazines would pick up on this as well?
Surely now they would be asking for more information?
Or maybe they will just draw their own conclusions?

Surely now the entire viewing public would be tuning in to The Factor? They will be keen to see the heartless slut that ditched her loyal devoted partner, for a sleazy fling with soccer's bad boy, on television casting judgement on other people as they auditioned for the show.

Photograph's of celebrities almost naked and the stories of their sleazy sex lives laid bare for everyone to see was what the public wanted, this was how you sold newspapers and magazines. Therefore this particular story of how the uncaring bitch had just discarded the man that had shown her 100% loyalty since the very first day they met, like he was just a used tissue, was a real scoop.

The previous day five bodies of British service personnel having been killed whilst on active service, had been flown into R.A.F Brize Norton, but that had only received a short paragraph on page eight.

Seven women and twelve children from an eastern European country had been found dead two days previously in the back of a container that had just arrived in Dover. They had asphyxiated.

The tragic story of their untimely deaths, just about made a quarter of a page somewhere near the middle.

The young blonde girl removed the towel from her well-toned body and let it drop to the floor, as she slid back into the bed beside him she proudly stated. 'I was on page three of that newspaper once.'

Powell was not in the slightest bit interested in her, the only thing on his mind right now was the amount of mileage he would gain from his recent publicity scheme.

'Not now Love, I'm busy, I have to leave now and I think

you had better go too.' Was the reply she received as Powell climbed out of bed and headed for the bathroom. 'What about my career? We were going to talk about it.' The young girl spoke to his naked backside.

As Powell slammed the bathroom door behind him, he replied. 'Oh yes that, good luck with it Love.'

He didn't call the attractive naïve young girl "Love" as a term of endearment. He called her "Love" because he did not know her name.

He had only just met her the night before at a glitzy party, otherwise known as a product launch for a national cosmetics company.

After a brief conversation in which she described her career. "I started off as a model, then somebody suggested I go into acting, so I thought why not? So that's what I am now an actress stroke model. Three months ago I started taking singing lessons, I'm getting quite good at it. I want to be a recording artiste. Of course I want to sing live as well. I can see myself onstage at the 02."

Powell then suggested. "I may be able to help you with your career. What do you say to us leaving this boring old party and going back to my hotel suite to discuss your future over a glass of champagne?"

She may have told him her name but he did not remember it was irrelevant to him, as he had no intention of ever seeing her again.

Powell stood there under the shower with the water cascading down his body feeling really pleased with himself and full of self-admiration.

He had done it, he had got his show back on the front pages. Surely now the viewing figures would increase substantially, back to how they had been before?

As she was putting on the clothes that she had worn the evening before, the pretty young blonde girl felt sickened as she realised that she had been taken for a complete fool. The arrogant Barstard that was older than her own father, had just spun her a yarn to coax her into being his plaything for the night and she had fallen for it. The only person she hated more than that scumbag in the bathroom standing under the shower right now was herself.

'How could I have been so stupid?' She cussed herself and was dreading the walk of shame she would have to endure as she returned to the three bedroom semi-detached house in a quiet suburban street that she shared with her parents. How many women would be wearing a midnight blue low cut silky cocktail dress and high heeled designer shoes at nine o'clock on a Tuesday morning?

Joseph was sat on the same sofa that he had spent so much happy contented time with Mellissa, just staring at the wall, feeling like the whole world had collapsed around him, to Joseph that is exactly what had happened, his whole world had collapsed.

Just a few miles away, sat another man, feeling alone and rejected.

Remorse

"The mobile number you have called is currently unavailable, please try again later."
Were the words that came from the pre-recorded message when Mellissa had called Joseph's mobile, as she was travelling in the car that was sent to pick her up and take her home from the airport.
She then tried to call their landline, but only received the engaged tone.
Mellissa felt a sense of relief, with the telephone being in use that must mean that Joseph would be at home, and she was longing to see him.
When she arrived at their home, there was no Joseph the home that they had shared was as usual spotlessly clean, without a single thing out of place apart from two broken telephones.
Looking around the room Mellissa noticed the photographs of Joseph had gone, when she looked in the wardrobes and the chest of drawers, she could not find a single item of his clothing.
The furniture was still in place, exactly as it was when she left. But her house no longer felt like a home, even though it was fully furnished it felt cold and bare.

On the coffee table there were yesterday's newspapers telling the sordid tale of her affair with "The bad boy of football." There was no love affair, there was no sexual encounter between then whatsoever.

There were only two people that knew that fact for sure herself and the premiership footballer Abdikarim Dalmar. When they arrived at Toulon-Hyeres airport they were greeted by a smartly dressed chauffeur and driven to a luxury villa on an exclusive complex in Saint Tropez. There they had separate en-suite rooms and when inside the villa had a minimal amount of contact with each other. Their instructions were "Whenever you are in the public eye you are to behave as if you are a couple of people enjoying a holiday together. Your goal is to attract the maximum amount of media attention that you possibly can. The purpose is to gain as much publicity as you can for the forthcoming series of The Factor."

Despite the fact that it was just a few days in the sun, it was a short break that the majority of people dream about. They dined in the best restaurants, spent their days on the beach and wherever they went they were chauffeur driven in a luxurious limousine.

But Mellissa did not enjoy it, she had no common interest with Abdikarim, the only interest he has is football, a sport she has no interest in at all, therefore they could find nothing to talk about, they very quickly became bored with the company of each other.

The paparazzi followed them everywhere they went taking photographs of them whenever they were away from the villa. She knew this was what Powell had planned, she expected this, but she disliked it strongly.

She was constantly thinking about Joseph, but her instructions were not to contact him until she had arrived back in the UK. Mellissa would then explain that to him and that she was just acting her part.

She had previously explained to him that with everything he saw her do on the television, and in every picture and article he saw of her in the newspapers and magazines she was just playing her role, like she was playing her part in a full length feature movie and none of it was the real Mellissa. When she cried in front of the television camera's as a cute little boy sang "I want to go to Heaven for the weekend." A song about a seven year old boy wanting to visit his daddy that had passed away, it was crocodile tears she was crying, the effect of that action was that thousands of television viewers wept along with her and the song went to number one in the UK charts. She also explained to him the reason why she had taken off all of her clothing in full view of eleven housemates and hundreds of thousands of T.V viewers, before they had met was. "The producers instructed me to do it to improve the viewing figures, they told me it would launch my career."

The real Mellissa was not an exhibitionist.

Apart from Joseph, Mellissa had only one other lover a lad she met when she was eighteen years old and had been in a relationship with for five years. That ended when he came out of the closet as he said. "I will always love you with all of my heart, but we cannot go on like this, I am living a lie, I am gay, I hope you understand."

Mellissa did understand, even though she was heartbroken, she understood Martin's feelings and they remain friends.

She is a genuine, loving, caring person and nothing like the girl she was made to look publicly.

The puppeteer pulls the strings, and Mellissa does the dance.

But now she felt that it had all gone too far.

Mellissa called the company Joseph was employed at and she was told "He has not attended the office today, when you speak to him can you tell him to call us immediately?"

She then called the canine sanctuary where he was a volunteer, they had not heard from him.

She then called his mother, the response she received to, "Hello Mrs Reynolds, this is Mellissa, is Joseph there?" Upset her immensely. "Don't you dare come near me or my son ever again you no good Trollope."

There was nowhere else for her to turn, she could not contact him and he had made no attempt to contact her. Joseph was no longer a part of her life, the feeling of remorse that she felt at this moment was nothing like she had ever experienced before.

Burke And Hare
The Story Behind Amellia

Giles Jefferson a university law graduate was appointed as
spin doctor for Power-Man Productions. Powell had set
him the task of taking care of George Answell,
Chlamydia, Amellia and the twins.
His instructions were to take to take their background
stories as far as he could possibly take them.
To maximise the publicity.
Without there being any redress to Power-Man
Productions or Trenton Powell himself.
Amellia was the one that caught his eye the most, having a
pretty young drug dealer on the show was a coup in itself.
She was also gutsy, feisty and exhumed an extreme air of
confidence, for a person so young. But lying below the
surface there was bundles of vulnerability.
Jefferson felt that her story was more open to exploitation
than that of anybody else on the forthcoming series.
So Jefferson began by looking into her parent's
background. He wanted to discover what it was that they
had done to turn their daughter against them. What
Skeletons! Did they have in their cupboard? He dug deep
but there was nothing he could use.
Amellia's mother and father had now been happily
married for twenty two years, neither one of them had ever
had an affair, they had no debts, they have no vices,

neither one of them had ever been in any trouble whatsoever and there were no criminal records to find. They were both hard working and were good loving parents to their only child.

So the angle he would use would be how the spoilt brat from a respectable background with loving doting parents that would have gladly given their whole lives for her, had turned bad, then left home and coldheartedly not cared one tiny little bit about the heartbreak and suffering that she had caused her parents.

To help him put Amellia's story together he had his assistant and sidekick Jennifer. Who despite only being twenty four years of age was fast becoming a big noise in the Power-Man enterprise. This was due to the fact that she had absolutely no scruples whatsoever and she was just as likely to publicly tell the truth as a politician fighting an election campaign.

Their first step was to paint a picture of Amellia.

At the age of thirteen Amellia would steal money from her mother's purse in order to buy alcohol and cigarettes, she would regularly stay out until the early hours of the morning and some nights would not return home until the following afternoon. At the age of fourteen she contracted a sexually transmitted disease and she also fell pregnant but due to alcohol abuse and the taking of un-prescribed drugs after three months the unwanted pregnancy ended, she had a miscarriage.

Her parents were at the end of their tether. They had always enjoyed a close relationship with their daughter, but in the last eighteen months she had become very distant and she treated them with contempt.

The only thing in their lives that mattered to them was their little girl. So they decided to put their house up for sale, and in their desperation to move away from the area in which they lived as quickly as possible they accepted an offer that was way below the initial asking price, which meant that they had to increase the borrowing on their mortgage as the property they had bought cost them £100.000 more than they had received for their home that they had sold, despite the fact that the house they would be moving into to was not any bigger or better than the one that they had sold. The reasoning behind accepting such a substantial loss was that they felt if they moved to another area it would give Amellia a fresh start away from the local youths that they were sure were leading her astray. Despite the financial difficulties this brought upon her parents, whilst the sale was going through they took her on a holiday of a lifetime.

When Amellia was a very young child she loved to watch her favourite animated film about a clown fish. If she watched the D.V.D once, she watched it a thousand times. This developed a fascination for sea life and so her parents Peter and Diana decided that a scuba diving holiday in the Maldives would be ideal.

Their plan seemed to be the solution. Amellia got back the fun loving child that was inside of her.

Every morning throughout the holiday she awoke excited with a fresh zest for life. The underwater camera that her father bought for her proved to be an absolute joy, each day she took hundreds of pictures of marine life, then she would spend the evening viewing them on her laptop and excitedly explaining them to her parents.

Diana and Peter were now happy and contented, they had got their little girl back.

They returned home from their holiday eight days before the house completion was due to go through and everything in the garden was rosy.

Amellia was back to her old self and they felt like a family again.

Then two days before they were due to move home Amellia was gone and all of her personal possessions had gone along with Diana's mother's wedding ring and the gold watch that Peter's father had given him.

Jefferson and Jennifer gave each other a jolly good pat on the back, they were delighted with the background story they had put together for Amellia. Not all of it is was entirely true, some of it was gross exaggeration, with a little bit of pure fabrication thrown it to spice the story up a bit. After all as the saying goes "Don't let the truth get in the way of a good story."

Amellia like all participants had signed a release form, so there good be no legal redress.

'I think we deserve a jolly good drink.' Said Jefferson to Jennifer.

Golden Girl

There was nobody in the office, Mellissa had been
instructed to be there at 10 O'clock sharp on Tuesday
morning. She was feeling really low and as there was
nobody present, she just stood there gazing through the
window. She never heard the turn of the door handle or the
footsteps approaching her. She turned her head and looked
to her side when Nicola asked. 'Mellissa are you Okay?'
'Yes I'm fine thank you.'
'You don't look fine in fact never before have I seen you
so upset.'
The tears were welling up in Mellissa's eyes as she
answered. 'He is always hugging me and kissing me and
telling me how much he loves me. But I think it's all over,
I don't think he ever wants to see me again.'
'Do you mean your boyfriend Joseph?'
Mellissa did not answer she just nodded her head as the
tears rolled down her cheeks.
'What happened? Have you had a fight?' Asked Nicola.
'No I haven't seen Joseph or spoken to him since
Thursday morning.'
'Why didn't he call you?'
'He couldn't call me, Mister Powell had my phone, the
chauffeur that picked me up from Stanstead airport gave it
back to me when we I got into the car. I was hoping that
Joseph would be at the airport to meet me. I wanted to

speak with him. I wanted to explain why I went away for the weekend without saying goodbye.'

'Was he not at the airport to meet you?'

'No how could he be there? I never told him I was going anywhere, or where I was going, or who I was going with and neither had I told him when I was coming back. So no Joseph was not at the airport to meet me. Nobody told him anything about it.'

The media were informed of Mellissa's arrival time and as Powell had planned, the welcoming party as she passed through the arrivals gate were hordes of photographers waiting like a pack of hungry wolves to snap her and Abdikarim together.

There were also a large number of reporters keen to speak with them.

Nicola was sympathetic. 'It must have been terrible for you.' She said.

'It was the worst experience of my life, the reporters stood in my way, they would not let me pass, and they were shouting things like "How long have you two been together?" And "Are you planning on setting up home together?" I didn't reply, I just called out "Can somebody help me?" The footballer seemed to be enjoying the attention, he was posing for the photographers and instead of helping me to get away he kept pulling me towards him. He was answering the questions the journalists were asking. I never heard what he said. There was so much noise. After what seemed like a lifetime the chauffeur and the airport security guards came and got me and as they were helping me to get away, one of the reporters shouted

"When did you realise you were pregnant?" Then he shouted "Who is the Father" I never replied I just wanted to get away from them as quickly as I could.'

'Are you pregnant?' Nicola asked.

'No of course I'm not, I don't even know how the rumour started.'

Nicola's voice had a touch of anger present as she asked.

'Why do you let him treat you like this?'

'He has always treated me so well, ever since the first time we met at the animal shelter. Joseph is so sweet.'

'I'm not talking about Joseph, I am talking about Powell, Trenton bloody Powell. I have heard the way he speaks to you and I have seen how he forces you to do things against your will, he walks all over you and treats you like dirt, like you're just a plaything for him to use and abuse.'

As she was choking back the tears Mellissa responded.

'No he is not a bad person you don't know him like I do.'

Nicola was surprised that her colleague had jumped to Powell's defence. She had never heard anyone say a nice thing about him before. He was the most despised man that she had ever met.

'I know that misogynistic, self-righteous, self-opinionated, no good shit bag only too well.'

Mellissa shook her head as she said. 'No you don't know him, nobody really knows him. After I got this job my mother told me ....'

She never finished her sentence.

Powell entered the studio, he could not have heard Nicola voice her opinion of him.

Looking like the cat that got the cream and carrying a copy of one of the daily tabloid papers.

He brushed Nicola aside as he praised Mellissa. 'Who's my little golden girl? I knew you could do it, I knew you would pull it off, the media are all over it, you're in every tabloid, on the front page of four of them and they were talking about you on the radio this morning, your affair with the footballer has really grabbed everybody's attention. You're not pregnant are you?'

'No I am not pregnant.'

Powell smirked to himself as he said. 'I wonder who started that rumour.'

Mellissa wiped the tears from her cheeks as she stated. 'And nothing happened.'

'What do you mean nothing happened?'

'We didn't sleep together, there was no sexual contact between us whatsoever.'

'Are you telling me that you spent a long weekend in Saint Tropez with a man and you didn't even shag him?'

'Of course I didn't, I love Joseph so much, and I would never be unfaithful.'

Powell did not inquire as to what it was that had upset Mellissa so much as to cause tears to flow from her eyes. He was not interested.

Due to her little trip to Saint Tropez his show was now the main topic throughout the media and nothing else mattered right now as he explained his excitement to his distraught assistant. 'It doesn't matter whether you shagged his brains out or not, as long as everybody thinks you did, that is all that counts. And the pictures you really are a gem, look at this one of you paddling in the sea, that is priceless, you really did catch the photographers eye, I knew your cute little arse would pay dividends one day, the viewing figures will soar.'

As he said "arse" Powell put his hand on her buttocks and began to slowly rub them.

This sickened Nicola so much that she left the studio, because Mellissa made no attempt to pull away or remove his hand from her body. She just said. 'He has left me.'

'Who's left you?'

'Joseph he's left me, and according to his mother he never wants to see me again.'

'Well that's what I call a result.'

'I love him.'

Whether or not Powell heard her statement of love for Joseph, nobody knows, did he choose to ignore it?

Did he simply just not hear it?

Was he aware that tears of sorrow filled her eyes?

The only thing that anybody could have been sure of was that he simply did not care.

He carried on speaking without any consideration for her whatsoever. 'It looks like Mary-Anne is going to come up trumps as well, what I need you to do is take her under your wing, we will dress her in the appropriate clothing. I want you to introduce her to the top London nightspots. As soon as she walks through the door of any club I want a bottle of champagne thrust into her hand. Get her intoxicated but not falling down drunk. It is important for her to be seen out and about having a good time, I will inform the paparazzi of your whereabouts, they are all loving you at the moment, so it won't be difficult to get them interested. It's also important that we get her seen engaging with the right people, the playboys and the bad lads, she's got the looks, all we need to do is throw a bit of gossip into the mixer and she will be a dead certainty to make the pages. Do you know right now my own photographer is absolutely loving her? He says "She is so photogenic, every shot is pure beauty." But we have come across a slight problem, she is refusing to have any shots of her taken unclothed. I need pictures of her with her tits outs for the Lads Mags. That is where you come in. I want you to go over to the hotel and convince her to take her clothes off for the camera. Explain to her that posing topless is no big deal, tell her about how it helped you with your career. Explain to her that nudity is the most natural thing in the world and it's nothing to be embarrassed about. I don't want to suggest it myself in case she thinks I am trying to manipulate her. I'm relying on you so don't let me down. And I need you to help us to separate her from her backward brother, Graham's doing the best he can, but he just ain't quite there, I might have to let him go. So there we have a nice little job for you, the car will take you to the hotel now. When you get there I want you to become Mary-Anne's best friend. I've got things to do here this morning, so I'll see you there later this afternoon. Oh! And one more thing, that little slut you were talking to when I came in, tell her she's sacked, I don't want to see her ugly face ever again.'

Digging The Dirt

Jefferson and Jennifer began researching George
Answell's past, the search proved to be faultless, however
far they looked, however many questions they asked, they
could not seem to find any background information on
Answell. They were also looking for the victim's family,
but nothing seemed to lead to them. Even their contacts in
the police force had nothing to offer. 'It must be because
manslaughter is such a serious offence. That has got to be
why his records are out of our reach.' Said Jefferson.
'I have an amazing idea for a background story.' Offered
Jennifer.
Jefferson replied. 'There really is no need, having a man
on The Factor that has just recently been released from
prison for killing another man is a scoop in itself. We can
go with the story as Answell himself told it. Then when it
goes on air I have no doubt that new angles will evolve,
people that know of his past are bound to come forward,
and we can make the story bigger as the show progresses.'
Jennifer nodded in agreement, then added. 'I don't think
we should have anybody mention manslaughter. He killed
the man is the point we need to put across, then the public
will presume that is was murder. Murder is much more
sensational.'
Jefferson agreed wholeheartedly then said. 'Right now
let's do Mary-Anne. What have we got on Mary-Anne?'
'Nothing.'

'What do you mean nothing?'

'Exactly that nothing. I dug as deep as I could and I came up with nothing.' Answered Jennifer.

'What about boyfriends? A hot bit of totty like that must have a string of boyfriends.'

'There are no boyfriends, I dug deep. No boyfriends.'

Jefferson looked quizzical as he asked. 'Are you saying that she is batting for your side? Are you saying she's a lesbian?'

'I wish.' Answered Jennifer with a sigh. 'No she is not batting for my side as you so elegantly put it. Mary-Anne is totally devoted to her twin brother, she has no time for anybody else.'

'Powell will insist on there being a story of her sex life thrown in.' Jefferson said. 'We will have to take her out get her drunk and get her laid.'

When looking into the background of Chlamydia they found it was an interesting one. He was born Reginald Albert Robinson, the only child of Frederick and Violet Robinson. As a child he was what one would describe as a normal healthy growing boy. At the age of Twenty Three Reginald married twenty eight year old Tracey and they had two children Daniel now aged eleven and Hannah aged nine.

Tracey was not aware of Reginald's passion for cross dressing until a couple of years prior to his audition for The Factor. That day she had arrived home earlier than expected. The children were at school, Tracey crept into the house with the view to surprising him, she was surprised to see Reginald in full women's dress and make-up admiring himself in front of a full length mirror. Tracey stood there silently, with her heart pounding and her face flushed.

A heated confrontation followed with Chlamydia blaming his wife Tracey for the reason why he had kept it from her. "You know what you are like, if I had told you when I wanted to you would have flown off the handle like you are doing now. You have never tried to understand me. I am not a man, I am a woman, accept that. You are married to a woman."

Tracey burst into tears as she screamed. "You are the father of my children you fucking freak." Then she stormed out of the house.

A couple of days later they sat down together and discussed the matter calmly, with Chlamydia explaining that he has always known that he was a woman trapped in a man's body and as soon as he could afford too, he would have the operation to change his gender.

From then on Chlamydia dressed and behaved as a woman, twenty four hours a day and urged the children to address him as "Mum, Mother or Mummy."

Tracey and Chlamydia decided that for the sake of the children they should stay living together under the same roof, although they slept in separate bedrooms and never again had any physical contact with each other.

So Jefferson and Jennifer, or "Burke and Hare" as the rest of the crew referred to them, due to the fact that it was their job to dig the dirt and bring up any old skeletons that they could find. Set out to sensationalize the background stories as much as they possibly could.

Conditioning

They all had their mobile phones taken away from them.
All of the televisions and radios in the hotel had been
removed.
The key participants in the Forthcoming series of The
Factor were not allowed to read any newspapers or
magazines. They were to have no communication with the
outside world whatsoever.
 Most of them would not be permitted to leave the hotel
until after the series had been aired, apart from the journey
that they would make to and from the 02 arena where the
series would be filmed when it went live.
 If it were necessary for any of them to leave, they were to
be chaperoned at all times.
It was explained to them that the reason was, so that "They
would be prepared for the stardom that awaited them."
Of course nobody complained, the way they all saw it was
that they were now living the dream. It was fame that they
were seeking. And fame was the carrot being dangled.
Chlamydia had his own personal assistant, a painfully thin
six foot two inch lad named Lynsey, who was as camp as
a row of pink tents and like Chlamydia he also had a
passion for cross dressing.
Although Chlamydia insisted that he was not a cross
dressers. "I am a woman and so I dress as a woman." He

would say assertively. If anybody dared to call him a transvestite or a cross dresser.

And so Lynsey and Chlamydia became good friends. They would while away the days and nights experimenting with make-up and trying on different outfits of which they were supplied an endless amount of.

Amellia was serious about her singing, she wanted to do nothing other than rehearse and so she was assigned her own personal voice coach.

Amellia was also given a supply of un-prescribed, which neither Trenton Powell or anyone on the payroll of Power-Man Productions knew anything about.

They could not be seen to be providing anyone with any form of illegal substance.

Bad publicity for the contestants was good for the show. But for Powell to be seen supplying un-prescribed drugs that was a no no.

There were two dance troupes, one an eight piece boy group in their twenty's. They performed under the name of "The Boys Stand Proud." Burke and Hare described them as "The Downtown Boys."

They came from working class backgrounds and even though they were good lads, a couple of them whilst they were in their teens had minor brushes with the law.

This was something that Burke and Hare intended to capitalise on.

The other troupe of dancers were eight young ladies that met when they were attending a private school for girls, they came from privileged backgrounds.

One of the girl's father's was a high court judge.

The eight girls were all stunningly good looking and spoke the Queen's English.

They called themselves "The Dancing Panthers."

Burke and Hare referred to them as "The Uptown Girls."

Both groups were supplied with countless amounts of alcohol and were instructed to get together to just enjoy themselves and party like there is no tomorrow.

Burke and Hare were hoping that as a result of the alcohol loosening inhibitions, coupled with having not much else to do, that they would be plenty of fornicating between the two groups, as they felt that there would be a few good stories for the press to be had there.

George Answell did not require any conditioning. "I just want to sit here quietly and read my books like I did when I was in prison." Was his answer when he was asked. "What can we do to help you?"

So even though a close eye was kept on him, he was pretty much left to his own devices.

Graham had his hands full with Sebastian, despite the fact that he was well behaved and was in Utopia putting together his enormous train set, of which he was being constantly supplied more track and trains for, along with the miniature buildings, trees and farmyard animals for making his lay-out.

He was constantly asking for his sister Mary-Anne.

She was still in the same building, Powell wanted extra attention paid to her, he felt that Mary-Anne would be a major player in the success of his forthcoming series.

Therefore he was not pleased that it was never possible for a couple of hours to pass by without anybody that was working with her having to halt what they were doing so that the twins could see each other.

Then he realised that the key to controlling Mary-Anne was to convince her that, his main concern was Sebastian's welfare.

She was told. "We have a team that are fully trained and experienced in dealing with people that have similar conditions as Sebastian and he will greatly benefit from the care that he will receive."

Mellissa arrived at the hotel and succeeded where everyone else on the Power-Man team had failed.

Within just a couple of hours of her arrival she had managed to persuade Mary-Anne to pose unclothed for the camera. She also managed to convince her by gentle persuasion that. "It would be good for Sebastian if the two of you spent some time apart, as it would encourage him to socialise with other people, he is already becoming more confident. He is really beginning to blossom and gain some independence. Look how well he is getting on with Graham."

Mellissa strongly disliked manipulating people in this manner, but she knew that the only way she could stay employed with Power-Man Productions was by delivering whatever Powell asked for.

The First Audition?

The first programme of the new series was going to be shown on channel five at 4 pm.

They were recording it today, then it would be cut and edited and shown on T.V the following week.

This was what the television audience were led to believe was the first audition, of course it wasn't, anybody that appeared on the televised show had already been auditioned at least once. But Powell and company had kept up the pretence of not knowing anything about the acts they saw on the first programme of a new series ever since The Factor had begun.

Powell was not at all happy that his show had been relegated to the afternoon slot on channel five, but he was feeling confident that with the new idea's he was putting into practice, coupled with the exciting characters that were being introduced, he would be able to generate enough publicity to bring in the number of viewers that the show needed to get back to prime time viewing on British television's most watched channel.

The setting was the packed 02 arena.

All of the complimentary tickets had been taken.

Somehow Powell managed to find enough people that still believed his show had some kind of significance to fill the vast venue.

Free tickets were issued to anyone that called the premium rate number and gave their name address and the number of tickets they required.

The telephone call took a minimum of four and a half minutes and cost the caller at the very least eleven pounds. The auditorium lights went down and Paul the larger than life T.V warm-up man, wearing his multi-coloured suit, bounced onto the stage and entertained the audience for twenty minutes with a blast of one liner gags.

He then loosened up their inhibitions with a few catchy sing-along numbers.

As he left the stage the audience were introduced to twenty five crew members that were positioned around the arena. They each wore brightly coloured red and yellow polo shirts and had some daft looking apparatus fixed to heads that shone a beam of light on them.

The audience were told to "Watch for when their lights went on and listen for their leads."

They then went on to lead the crowd with some chanting followed by a few minutes of random booing and cheering.

Then music was blasted around the arena and the crowd were treated to an amazing light show, better than anything any of them had ever seen before.

The audience were then instructed to stand and cheer and scream with excitement.

They did this without anyone questioning why?

They were enjoying being swept along with the enthusiasm.

Then the introduction was blasted around the venue.

"Welcome to a brand new series of The Factor. Here he is the man that makes the dreams come true. The showbiz legend himself Mister Trenton Powell."

The doors positioned dead centre at the back of the stage slid open and smoke was coming up from the floor as he walked through them with his smug self-praising smile, the audience were already on their feet cheering with gay abandonment as the T.V cameras scanned around the auditorium giving the effect that they had stood up and were applauding Powell.

Mellissa followed, she looked stunning dressed in a deep red full length cocktail dress.

Then came Lewis Marshall, as he walked out the music faded and so did the applause as everyone sat down.

The show's presenter was introduced by an offstage announcement and as he took to the stage, he was welcomed by a massive round of applause.

The three judges sat at an oblong table Mellissa sat in the middle with Powell on one end and Marshall on the other.

Marshall was sixty eight years of age, he was slim, with thinning grey hair, he spoke with a soft southern Irish accent and like Powell he had no experience of working in the field of entertainment before the days of The Factor.

Marshall was a judge on The Factor in the early days but hadn't been connected with the show for five years, until Powell called him out of the blue to invite him back.

Powell and Marshall had very little in common apart from the fact that they both possessed an oversized ego.

And on the plus side Marshall had a brother that was a major shareholder within a large publishing company that produced weekly gossip magazines.

Therefore sensing that having Marshall back on-board would get the show back in the gossip mags Powell had invited him to join him in the new series at the judges table.

The two of them were always polite and courteous to each other, despite the fact that each one strongly disliked the other.

One day Marshall overheard Powell referring to him as. "That thick Irish Twat."

He never made any comment and neither was he bothered, as he himself when talking about Powell would refer to him as. "That big headed arrogant Prick."

Whenever they addressed each other it was as "Lewis" and "Trenton."

The first auditionee to step onto the stage was one of the misfits. It was always a good idea to open a new series with a misfit.

The footage on this particular misfit was brief as they found no skeletons in her cupboard and Powell had already decided that she would not be selected to go through to the next round. Therefore there was no need to build her character up.

The short film that preceded the sixty five year old lady's appearance onstage showed her sat at home dressed in a one piece leopard print catsuit surrounded by no less than thirty seven cats. They were climbing all over her and all over the furniture. As one watched the spectacle on the screen, one could almost smell the cat's urine.

When she walked onto the stage, she was dressed as a tiger, she did not introduce herself. She just burst into song as she sang the sixties Lulu classic. "I'm a Tiger."

It sounded dreadful and the way she pranced around clawing at fresh air looked absolutely ridiculous.

The audience were encourage to chant "Off" "Off" "Off" When the Catwoman had finished it was Mellissa that spoke first. 'Well that was certainly different, but I don't think it is what we are looking for today.'

Then it was Powell's turn to comment. 'That has got to be by far the worst audition we have ever had since The Factor first begun.'

Powell had uttered those exact words to hundreds of hopefuls over the years but he never got tired of saying them. It gave him some kind of sadistic pleasure.

Although it did nothing for his personal popularity, it did help to increase the viewing figures.

Then it was Marshall's turn to speak, this was why the crew dreaded his return to The Factor, because it always took him ten minutes to say what any normal person would say in ten seconds.

He began in his usual patronizing manner. 'I have absolutely no idea why it is that you are here today. You definitely cannot sing and you are totally void of any kind of talent whatsoever, and I am baffled as to why it is you are dressed as a Tiger. I would say that however you choose to dress, it would not make any difference, as I would not vote you through to the next round because ....'

He was not permitted to finish, the Catwoman cut in.

'That's because you are a fucking arsehole. And I have no idea why you are here today you fucking arsehole, you can go and fuck yourself.'

As she finished speaking she turned to walk from the stage, as she did so she pointed her index finger upwards whilst staring at Marshall.

Powell was delighted, that was an excellent start. A totally ridiculous looking woman with a fetish for cats using foul abusive language, which was aimed at Marshall.

He loved and he knew his viewing public would love it.

The second person to be shown was George Answell. They had filmed him walking away from the gates of a London prison with a rucksack on his back.

When he walked onto the stage Powell asked him to. 'Tell us about yourself. And what are you hoping to get from today's audition?'

When Answell answered there was a strong lack of confidence in his voice. 'My name is George. I am a delivery driver. I am hoping that today's audition will result in me making a career as a singer.'

Powell nodded his head as he said. 'Go on. Good luck.'

When Answell began to sing for the first few seconds there was total silence in the auditorium.

The audience were blown away by his pitch perfect voice. Then they erupted with massive applause.

When Answell finished everybody in the venue including the judges was on their feet applauding.

When the applause faded, it was Marshall that spoke first. 'I really really liked that. You definitely have got The Factor, never before have I heard anyone sing so faultlessly. You definitely have ....'

Powell cut in. 'That was marvellous, exactly what we are looking for.'

'Thank you.' Replied Answell.

When Mellissa spoke, she did so with a beaming smile. 'You have blown the entire audience away that was incredible.'

Powell then said. 'Okay let's vote.'

Mellissa. 'It's a yes from me.'

Powell. 'And a yes from me.'

Marshall. It's a yes from me. You really are ...'

Powell cut him off. 'So that's it three yesses, you are through to the next round.'

Answell said. 'Thank you.'

As he turned to walk away Powell asked. 'Just out of curiosity, why were you filmed standing outside a prison?'

Answell answered coyly? 'I have just been released from prison.'

'What the earth for?' Asked Marshall.

'I did four years, for killing a man in ...'

Marshall cut in. 'Oh! Sweet Mary mother of Jesus. How did you get on the show? We can't have a ....'

Powell stood up, he was waving his arms in the air as he bellowed. 'If only I knew I would never have had you on the show. But we have voted now and we cannot go back on our word.'

'Cannot go back on our word.' Marshall repeated. 'Cannot go back on our word. The man is a murderer for pity's sake. Too right we can go back on our word.'

'We voted the man through to the next round, so he is through to the next round.' Said Powell assertively.

The auditorium was silent, the audience were stunned. Some of them were big fans of The Factor and they had seen enormous amounts of crazy people, that was the attraction, that was why they watched the show, but never before had they seen a murderer.

Jason the head cameraman broke the silence. 'I think we need to take a ten minute break.' He called out, then he took Powell into a side room.

Inside the room Powell was ecstatic, this was perfect. Marshall's reaction was much better than he had hoped for. It was well worth having that stupid old git on the show. And as for the audience, their stunned silence said more than a thousand words.

Whilst Powell and the crew were taking a break, on the big screens the audience in the 02 were shown footage from the highlights of previous shows.

Twenty five minutes had passed before Powell and Jason emerged from the side room.

The cue was given and the on the giant screen came footage of Chlamydia, he was at home with his children, and he was seen explaining to them. "From now on you are not to call me Dad. I am not a man I am a woman." Then Chlamydia walked onto the stage looking every inch a woman. A great big giant of a woman.

He introduced himself and explained. "I am a woman locked in a man's body and success on this show, will give me the finances to release from this hell that I am trapped in." He then recited his poem. It was humiliating, the audience that normally love to laugh and mock the misfits, felt embarrassed for him.

When he finished it was Marshall that spoke first. 'I love your enthusiasm, I love your passion. You obviously perform with your entire heart and soul, but I do not think that you have what we are looking for. The Factor is about talent and you do not ......'

Powell cut in. 'I think you have made your point Lewis. And surprise surprise for once I agree with you.'

All eyes were now on Mellissa, she spoke with an uneasy tone in her voice. 'I am afraid I don't think you have what it takes ....'

She did not finish, Chlamydia burst into tears, through the sobbing he pleaded. 'Please. Please give me a chance. I will do anything' As two burly security lads escorted him from the stage into view of a T.V camera that was waiting to film him in the wings.'

So that was that Chlamydia's dream was over and Powell would milk his humiliation as much as he could.

Amellia was filmed in a filthy squat, there were hypodermic needles littering the floor and she was seen rolling a large cigarette.

She walked onto the stage wearing torn black denim jeans and a black short sleeved T-shirt. She told them about her drug dealing lifestyle and about how she had left home without telling her parents. Then she sang.

When Amellia finished singing it was Marshall that spoke first. In his usual condescending manner. 'My child you really do have an exceptional singing voice, but here at The Factor we are role models for the youth of today. Therefore I feel that if we were to put you through to the next round of the show, we would be sending out the wrong message about the way we feel towards the taking of illegal drugs, and that really would not do, so I am afraid I am going to have to say no. No. Absolutely no way can we put you through to the next round.'

Marshall paused to take a breath.

Powell saw this as an opportunity to cut in. 'When I see someone like yourself with all the talent you have has gone astray, I feel that a superior force has brought you to me in order for me to help you, and help you is what I intend to do. I will take you to boot camp and pay for you to receive the best professional treatment available, to help you kick the drug habit and lead a clean healthy lifestyle.'

The applause that followed Powell's statement was deafening. Powell was in his element, they actually believe that he genuinely wants to help the poor girl.

Just like the fools that tune in to see his pal Jezza Lyle, think that his freak show is there to help.

Mellissa spoke next. 'I am here to judge you on your talent, not on your lifestyle. I believe you have got what it takes to make it big. You will go far.'

'Okay let's vote.' Said Powell. 'I say yes.'

Mellissa voted next. 'It's a great big yes from me.'

Then it was Marshall's turn. 'A thousand no's from me.' You should leave here now and go to a hospital right away or I shall call the police and have you ….'

Nobody heard anymore, the booing and the jeering was deafening. The crowd had turned against Marshall.

When the audience had quietened down, Powell said 'You are through to the next round see you at boot camp.' Amellia thanked him then skipped off.

The next act to appear was a young woman with her pet Vietnamese potbellied pig. The role of the pig was to complete the trails of a make-shift obstacle course that had been placed upon the stage.

The woman whistled the command, the pig did nothing, she repeated the command, again nothing. The crowd became amused by this, after five minutes of nothing happening, and lots of mocking from the audience, a highly embarrassed young lady, along with her pet pig were dismissed.

Then came what Powell believed was his masterpiece. Footage was shown of Mary-Anne and Sebastian. They were both casually dressed, they wore faded blue denim jeans, he wore a royal blue polo shirt and she wore a white crew neck t-shirt. To begin with they were shown walking through the park holding hands, then Mary-Anne was sat on a swing while Sebastian gently pushed her to and fro. Then they were shown sitting on the grass sharing a picnic, Sebastian looked deep into his sister's eyes and said "I love you." The next shot of them was at home holding a picture of their parents, with Mary-Anne saying. "We miss you so much."

Then hand in hand they nervously walked onto the stage. They were asked to talk about themselves. Mary-Anne spoke about their family background and the tragic story of how their parents were killed when they were just eleven years old.

A camera zoomed in on Mellissa as she wiped the tears from her eyes.

The twins then sung, it sounded beautiful, only it was not them that the audience heard singing, their voices were dubbed, it was a couple of session singers that everybody heard.

When they finished the three judges praised them and told them that they would be put through to the next round.

Powell then instructed Mary-Anne to look into the camera and speak.

'I don't know what to say.' She answered coyly.

Powell replied. 'That's okay, just look into the camera and read what it say's on the cue sheet.'

Mary-Anne did as she was instructed. 'Thank you Mellissa, this is what I always wanted. I don't care about anything other than my brother Sebastian. The only thing I want right now is for Sebastian and I to become successful and have a hit record.'

'That's excellent.' Said Powell. 'Now hold both of Sebastian's hands and recite the next sentence.'

Mary-Anne did so with compassion. 'Sebastian we will never each other again, you will be a pop star and I will be a pop star.'

Powell stood up and said. 'That is brilliant, now Sebastian you are overcome with emotion, look at Mary-Anne and say "No" as if you don't believe your luck, then throw your arms around her and put your head on her shoulder and sob as if you are totally overcome with emotion.'

Without hesitation Sebastian did as he was instructed.

When they finished filming and the auditorium was cleared Powell instructed Mellissa to 'Look into the camera and read what it says on the cue card.'

Mellissa did so without hesitation. 'Mary-Anne you have real talent but I am afraid I can only put you through to the next round if you drop your brother and go solo.'

Then Powell looked into the camera and said. 'I am afraid I have to agree with Mellissa, you have to go solo.'

Marshall was outraged, which was plain to see as he spoke out. 'I do not agree with you. It would be immoral to split them up. Besides they look sensational together. They are twins and they have always been inseparable. It is plain to see they love each other and the viewers will love.........'

He was not permitted to finish, Powell yelled at him. 'For fuck's sake will you shut up? You stupid gibbering cunt. Here I am trying to get the viewing figures up. I am trying to get us back on the top slot and that will not happen by being nice. No more mister nice guy.'

He then turned to the crew and said. 'I want the girl edited so that she is saying. "Thank you Mellissa, I don't care about my brother, the only thing I want is to become successful and have a hit record." Then she takes his hands and looks him in the eye and says. "Sebastian we will never see each other again and I will become a pop star." He just says "No" and sobs on her shoulder.'

So there it was cut and edited ready to be served up to the viewing public.

The Shaping Of Mary-Anne

The redesigning of Mary-Anne was almost complete.
Mellissa had managed to convince her to put her
inhibitions to one side and pose naked.
She refused to pose full frontal.
As Powell did not want full frontal nudity he was happy
with that. The exposure of her breasts and buttocks would
make this extraordinarily attractive young lady a certainty
to be featured in the lad's mags and on the third page of
some of the daily tabloids.
Now here she was stood before him after having a full
make over, with her hair and make-up looking
exceptionally glamorous.
Her clothes looked tacky and slutty.
She was wearing a very low cut top that exposed her
cleavage, it was also ten inches above her waistline
exposing her naval. The skirt she wore was so short that it
was barely more than a belt.
Despite her youth she was a picture of provocative
smouldering sexuality.
Not the way any parent would want their daughter her to
present herself. She looked like every young man's dream
and every father's nightmare.
Powell eyed Mary-Anne up and down, then he said
approvingly. 'Now that is the look I am going for, the
viewers will love it.'
Mary-Anne had never dressed this way before, whenever
she wore a skirt it always come down to her knee and

never before had she worn a top that was cut so low it exposed her cleavage.

At this moment, the way Powell was looking at her made her feel uncomfortable.

She replied sheepishly. 'I'm not sure this is not really me.'

Using all of the animation that he could in order to stipulate his point, Powell responded. 'You look absolutely amazing. Do you want to be a pop star? Then you need to look like one. Mellissa tell her how does she look?'

'Stunning, you look stunning.' Said Mellissa.

'Can I go to see Sebastian now?' Mary-Anne asked.

'Of course you can. Nobody would ever stop you from seeing your brother.' Answered Powell.

As Mary-Anne was walking through the hotel corridor on her way to conference room two, Powell turned to Mellissa and said. 'I have told you to split the two of them up. There is a car waiting outside to take the two of you to London. I want her dressed in the skimpiest of clothing at all times, I want her chaperoned everywhere she goes, I want her going to the top London nightspots. I want photographers following her everywhere she goes. Now don't just stand there get yourself tarted up. You have got ten minutes to make yourself look slutty.'

Fifteen minutes later Mellissa walked into conference room two.

The twins were happy and smiling as Sebastian was showing Mary-Anne how to work the controls on his electric train set.

Mellissa stood there watching them happily enjoying each-others company for a few minutes, then she said. 'We had better go now Mary-Anne, they are waiting to take us to London. Mister Powell has booked a suite for us in a top hotel.'

'I think it would be better if I stayed here with Sebastian.' Replied Mary-Anne.

Graham had just been standing back whilst Sebastian explained his lay-out to Mary-Anne. But now he felt he should speak. 'Sebastian is having a ball, you can see that for yourself. A couple of days apart will be good for you. When you come back your brother will show you how much bigger we can make the lay-out in just a few days. What do you think Sebastian? Should your lovely sister go to London for a couple of days?'

Sebastian looked Mary-Anne in the eye as he said. 'Yes go to London and have some fun.'

'Are you sure?' Asked Mary-Anne.

'Yes I am sure.'

'What will you do?'

'I will stay here with Graham and build my lay-out.'

Not another word was spoken, the twins hugged each other affectionately, then Mary-Anne turned and left the room with Mellissa.

As they closed the door behind them, Graham turned to Sebastian and said. 'Well done.'

'Did I say the right thing?'

'You did Sebastian. Well done.'

Sebastian burst into tears.

The Call

It was the call that Powell had been wanting and how he
relished every moment of it. But it was not the pompous,
smug, self-righteous Barstard that had previously told him
his show was being moved from the top slot who had
called him. It was a junior employee. "Mister Powell in
light of the enormous amount of publicity the show has
received, I have great pleasure in informing you that for a
trial period, the board have decided to move The Factor
back to the Saturday evening 8 p.m. slot that it previously
filled. We will of course confirm this by email."
The publicity was colossal, every single tabloid had
featured the show on the front page.
Each newspaper picked its favourite part of the show.
With the headline on one of the newspapers, with
reference to Amellia and Answell being.
"The Murderer and the Drug Dealer."
Amellia's story also made the television news
programmes. They repeated previously shown footage of
Amellia's parents when she had first disappeared, with
them pleading for anyone that knew anything of her
whereabouts to come forward.
Then footage was shown of them the morning after the
show was televised, shedding tears of relief, having
discovered that their daughter is alive and well.
The location of The Factor participants was kept secret.
Amellia's parents were desperately trying to contact her.
They made numerous calls to the television company and
the office of Power-Man Productions that proved to be

fruitless. They finally managed to speak with an employee who assured them that. "Amellia is being well cared for and is undergoing treatment to kick her drugs habit, we will arrange tickets for you for the 02 arena, for the filming of the next round of Factor 2025 in which Amellia is a contestant."

Whenever George Answell was mentioned in the papers or on the television magazine chat shows, the same question was asked every time. "Should a convicted killer be allowed on a television talent show?"

The icing on the cake was that the stories of Answell and Amellia. "The murderer and the drug dealer." Were even discussed on Prime Ministers question time.

Powell's favourite was Mary-Anne, he had personally engineered her publicity without any assistance from Burke and Hare.

She had made all of the weekly lad's mags and was featured on the third page of most of the daily tabloid papers.

He proudly and unashamedly boasted. "I have made that girl the most famous face in the whole of the United Kingdom. In fact I have also made her the famous piece of tits and arse as well. She has gone from being completely unknown to becoming an A list celebrity in the space of one week."

She was also featured in all of the women's weekly magazines. Every publication that she was in told the story of the good time girl that had turned her back on her loving brother with special needs, for a life of promiscuity and debauchery.

Back On Top

So here he was back on television's much sort after prime time slot.

It had worked, the background publicity behind his key players had generated so much interest in his show that it had to be there, back on top.

The audience were primed and the judges were in their place, waiting to give their verdict, like jumped up magistrates in a courtroom.

The lights went down and the first to appear on the big screen was George Answell. In the footage that was shown of him he was standing outside the prison gates telling the tale of how he had killed another man and how he had paid his debt to society. He then went on to say how grateful he was to Mister Trenton Powell for giving him the opportunity to appear on The Factor and make a new life for himself.

Then they showed footage of an unknown out of work actress that Power-Man Productions had employed.

Her role was to claim to be the wife of George Answell's victim. She had tear stained eyes as she said. "I am a Christian and I have tried so hard to forgive this man for killing my husband and the father of my children. But how can I do that when I cry myself to sleep every night, because I constantly have to explain to the little ones that their Daddy will not be coming home."

Then George Answell stepped onto the stage.

As he did so the audience booed so loudly it was deafening.

Above the noise from the crowd Answell heard the backing music coming from the monitor speaker that had been placed on the centre of the stage, facing up to him. Despite the heckling from the assembly in the packed arena Answell performed like a true pro.

The audience did not care, his singing was irrelevant to them, they had read about the killer and they had seen the footage of the dead man's widow talking about the grief that this man had brought to her family.

What he sang like was of no interest to them.

By the time he had finished the crowd were chanting.

"Off, off, off, off, off."

Powell stood up and gestured for the mob to stop.

The booing subsided and then Marshall spoke. 'There is no place for a murderer on this show. The fact is you killed a man and I do not believe that you deserve a second chance. Did you give the man you killed a second chance? Did you give his wife and children a second chance? No you didn't. Do you know that up until 1964 murder carried a compulsory death sentence in this country and you would have been hung by the neck until you were dead? Personally if I had my way you would still be in prison where you......'

'Hang the Barstard.' Shouted a member of the audience.

'I rest my case.' Said Marshall with a smug holier than thou look on his face.

Mellissa then spoke. Powell had briefed her on what to say. 'We are not here to judge you on anything that you have done in your personal life. We are here to judge your ability as a performer. As for myself. I think you have an amazing voice and....'

She was unable to finish. The audience were yelling.

"Hang him, hang him, hang him, hang him."

Powell was absolutely loving this. It was sensational.

He knew that the right thing to do was to keep Answell on the show.

When the jeering subsided. He said. 'This is a talent competition. My part in it is to decide whether or not you have got a sufficient amount of talent. I also have to take into consideration that the overall winner will be performing at The London Palladium in the Royal Variety Show before the King and Queen. So therefore I ask myself. Would it be appropriate for me to put a convicted killer on the show? One side of me says no. Then again if you were to make it to the final. I will not be judging, the phone in viewers at home will decide who the overall winner is. You have already been judged and sentenced by the court for the crime that you committed. So the question I ask is. Do I also judge you for your crime? Or do I judge you for your talent?' I think we should now vote. Lewis would you like to go first?'

'It's a thousand no's from me.' Said Marshall.

'Mellissa. What do you say?'

The reality of how delicate the situation was made Mellissa uneasy, it was evident by the tone of her voice.

'As Trenton has said you have already been judged by the court. Personally I believe that one day you will be judged by God Almighty.'

Powell interjected. 'Are you talking about me?'

Mellissa feigned a chuckle, as if she was impressed by a witty comment.

Then she carried on speaking. 'I am only qualified to judge you on your talent. So I will vote yes. I cannot judge you for your crime.'

'That's because you're a whore.' Shouted somebody in the audience.

'Go and shag the bad boy of football.' Yelled another.

The entire crowd then began chanting. "Slut, slut, slut."

Mellissa was reeling, she was heartbroken that her relationship with Joseph was over.

She needed medication to help her sleep at night.

She did not need reminding that it was the news of an affair that never was. That had caused the break-up of her relationship with the man that she had intended to spend the rest of her life with.

Powell was cherishing every moment of this.

His show was back on top and would now be a certainty to stay there.

When he spoke, he tried his hardest to sound humble. 'This is not what I wanted to happen. I was hoping that you two would vote the same, so that I would not have to decide whether or not a killer goes through to the next round. In order for me to leave here with a clear conscience this evening, I am going to decide on talent, and talent alone. So therefore my vote is yes. You are through to the next round.'

Answell thanked the judges and as he was leaving the stage the audience chanted. "Hang him, hang him, hang him, hang him."

Then followed a succession of four bum acts.

That was the term used by Powell and the Power-Man crew to describe a performer or a group of performers that were there purely as cannon fodder, they would not progress any further than the second round.

Their background stories were not strong enough.

So behind the scenes Powell and his team referred to them as "The Bum Acts."

Next to appear on the screen were Mary-Anne and Sebastian. It began with the two of them happy together, followed by the edited scene in which she appears to be telling Sebastian that she is now leaving him to go solo.

Then there were shots of her modelling unclothed, followed by footage of her dancing in a London nightclub with a muscular male dancer from a dance/strip troupe called Naughty Nights.

In her hand was a bottle of champagne.

The footage then went back to Sebastian who was crying as he said. "Mary-Anne where are you?"

This whole thing was cunningly crafted by Powell.

The scary thing is, it was not difficult.

Mary-Anne was on the dance floor with Mellissa, when she was given the thumbs up, she was to excuse herself and ask Mary-Anne to hold the champers for her.

Then the male stripper who was hired by Powell went and danced alongside Mary-Anne. This only lasted for a few seconds, but that was all that was needed to get the footage in the can.

From the moment that Mary-Anne had left her brother to go to London, they had no communication with each other. She could not call him as he had no mobile and whenever she enquired about him she was assured that he was being well looked after and was enjoying his time in the Dorset hotel.

It was not difficult to get Sebastian to breakdown and cry, after nearly a week of not seeing his sister, he was told.

"Mary-Anne won't be coming back, she doesn't love you anymore."

When Mary-Anne was introduced, the crowd that filled the 02 booed loudly but she did not take to the stage.

The backstage crew were frantically trying to locate her but to no avail. Nothing happened for a few minutes, so they decided to take a break.

Powell was livid, when he got backstage he did not hold his anger in.

'Where is she?' He bellowed at the wardrobe assistant.

'I don't know Mister Powell, Mary-Anne was here in her dressing room, I did her hair and her make-up, and then I excused myself and went to the bathroom and when I returned she was not here. I thought one of the backstage crew had taken her to the wings.'

He then turned his anger on the backstage crew. 'If you don't find that little tart pronto, you will be out of a job. Now don't just stand there, find her.'

Twenty five minutes had past and there was no sign of Mary-Anne.

So Powell decided to carry on filming without her, vowing that when they had finished heads would roll.

They began with three bum acts, an average male vocalist. Then a sword swallower that cut his throat on the inside and had to be rushed to A&E.

Followed by a thalidomide piano player.

Now it was time for Amellia.

A camera was fixed on her parents, as footage was shown of her talking about her unhealthy lifestyle.

Then she said. "I owe my life to Trenton Powell. He picked me up when I was on the floor. If it was not for that great man, I would not be here. I do not know what would have become of me."

Then she walked onto the stage, the music started and she began to sing a soft, sad ballad.

"I'm sorry so sorry, I didn't mean to make you cry…….."

As she sang tears were rolling down the faces of her parents. When she finished the song they ran onto the stage and hugged her in what looked to be the most emotionally charged reunion ever.

Powell got up from his seat and joined them on the stage. The audience were on their feet applauding and cheering enthusiastically, when the applause faded Powell spoke.

'You know it's at times like this when I feel that all of the hard work that I put into The Factor has been worthwhile.' Again the applause lifted, when it faded Amellia's parents thanked Powell for rescuing their little girl.

Amellia was voted through to the next round and as she was leaving the stage with her parents either side of her, with their arms around her shoulders, Powell looked into the camera and said. 'This is what The Factor is all about.'

Cherry Pie

Powell was feeling quite smug, The Factor was already back on top and with what he had in the can it was sure to stay there. No more talk of Thursday afternoon's on channel five.

At that moment Mary-Anne burst onto the stage her mascara was mixed with tears and was smeared across her face as she approached Powell and uncharacteristically screamed. 'Powell you Barstard, why did you do that to Sebastian?'

'Get her out of here.' Powell demanded, pointing his index finger from his outstretched arm towards the door.

Nobody made any movement towards the distraught young lady but all eyes were fixed upon her as she yelled. 'You said he would be looked after.'

Powell looked at her sternly and replied in a very cold matter of fact way. 'You knew what you were letting yourself in for, you wanted fame and you got it.'

'I didn't want this.' She sobbed.

Mellissa was now on the stage, she was really concerned as she asked the distraught young lady. 'Mary-Anne what has happened.'

'At first I thought he was just trying to make me look like a common slut, he certainly got me to dress like one. I could cope with that, but every time I tried to call Sebastian somebody from the Power-Man team answered the phone and told me that "He was enjoying himself and he wouldn't come to the phone as he was too busy." We have never been apart before.'

Mellissa trying to comfort Mary-Anne said. 'I'm sure if you want to see Sebastian Mister Powell will arrange that for you.' As she said those words a feeling of regrettable guilt ran through Mellissa, as her instructions were to keep the twins apart.

The tears were still flowing and even though her whole body was shaking. The tone of her voice was softer and more controlled as Mary-Anne stated. 'Whilst I was waiting in the dressing room the police came to see me and asked me if we could go somewhere where we would not be disturbed. We went into a quiet room. Then they showed me an article in this morning's newspaper about the good time girl that has totally rejected her poor, sweet, devoted brother and never wants to see him again. You really have succeeded in making me look like a cold hearted bitch.'

There was silence, nobody uttered a word.

All eyes were on Powell.

For the first time in his life he did not like being the focus of attention.

His back was against the wall as he answered defensively. 'You cannot blame me for that. I cannot be held responsible for what the newspapers print.'

The entire Power-Man crew did blame Powell for that. They knew that he was responsible for the manufacturing of the stories that were fed to the press.

Mary-Anne was now choking back the tears and the words came out slowly through the sobbing, as she said. 'The police told me that Sebastian was seen holding a newspaper and staring at it whilst he was crying out "Mary-Anne. Mary-Anne why don't you love me anymore?" Then he jumped under a train. We have killed Sebastian.'

Nobody spoke, there was deadly silence. Inside the 02 arena there were 20,000 people but you could have heard a pin drop. It was if the whole world had stopped moving. The only movement was the tears running down the face of Mary-Anne. Everybody else was frozen to the spot. It was Powell who broke the silence as he looked into the main camera being controlled by Jason and commanded. 'Cut that.' He then addressed the entire audience as he stated. 'I will remind you all that everything you have seen and heard here in this venue is strictly confidential and you are legally bound not to discuss this with any third party.'

Just then George Answell burst onto the set, he was full of anger, not the kind of anger that one might experience when returning to one's car and finding that some thieving Nazi Barstard has placed a parking fine on the windscreen. No this was deep down festering hatred, the love he felt for his daughter Natasha would never die, but she had, she had died at a young age from anorexia, brought on by Powell's "Too plump" jibe.

Followed by the humiliation of being conned and unwittingly playing a role in assisting of the conning of her friend's, by the parasite Farrington that called himself "Chris the Greek." Answell's beautiful daughter Natasha had lost the will to live.

Following his daughter's death Answell had gone to his local police station and told them about how Powell's remarks, followed by her being conned had led to his daughter Natasha's passing away.

The response he received from the police officer he spoke to was. "No crime has been committed by Mister Trenton Powell therefore we will not be taking any action against him. Farrington is known to us and is currently under investigation for fraud, but with have insufficient evidence to charge him with, therefore a forthcoming prosecution is highly unlikely."

Answell wanted revenge, the hatred he felt for Farrington and Powell was eating at him from the inside. When realising he would get no justice through the British legal system, he decided, to take the matter into his own hands. In a raised assertive voice that was full of rage Answell stated. 'There will be no cutting or editing of this show, they are not your film crew, they are my crew. The television audience will see and hear every single word that has been uttered, you are finished, people will finally be told the truth, and you will be thoroughly exposed.'

Powell looked down his nose at Answell as he said. 'Stop being silly, I pay the wages.'

Then he looked towards Jason as he said. 'Switch the camera's off. Let's clear the building and edit the show.' Then looking around the arena he said. 'That's it the show's over, I hope you all enjoyed the acting skills of the good time girl and the murderer, it's time to go home now.'

Nobody moved, except Jason he walked onto the stage, and declared. 'I am working without pay I would like to add, for Georgie, because he is a good man and you deserve to be exposed for all the heartache you have caused. Never mind the amount of nights I have laid awake with a broken my heart while you have been out gallivanting with some old slapper, Trenton Baby.'

Powell never said a word his bisexuality and his relationship with Jason was one of showbiz best kept secrets. Now Jason had turned against him and announced it to the world. Powell slapped his face as hard as he possibly could.

Jason cried. 'I loved you, you Barstard.'

George Answell was at breaking point, he launched himself at Powell as he yelled. 'I will destroy you, you scumbag.'

Mellissa forced herself between them, and pleaded in Powell's defence. 'No please don't do that.'

'You have nothing to worry about Mellissa. You have done nothing wrong.' Answell replied. 'But that scumbag will get what's coming to him.'

'He's not a scumbag, you don't understand, he is a good man.'

'How can you defend him? His callous remarks killed my daughter. And look at the way he treats you. He hates you, he hates everybody. I have been on to him for a while. How did you get your job?'

Mellissa was shaking her head as she said. 'He doesn't hate me. He doesn't hate…...'

Answell did not give her the chance to finish the sentence. He repeated the question. 'How did you get your job?'

'I auditioned and he said, "You are exactly the person that I am looking for." Then I started the following week.'

'How did you get your job?'

'He is a good man he ….'

'Forced you to have sex with him.' Answell bellowed.

For a few seconds there was an uncomfortable silence. Then Powell joined in the debate as he said defensively. 'I have never forced her to have sex with me, I have never forced anyone to have…...'

He didn't finish the statement, the way that Mellissa looked at him explained it all.

Of course Powell had not physically forced her to spend the night with him when she had applied for the job, although he had made it perfectly clear to her at the time that if she didn't, the position would have been offered to somebody else that would.

The night that she had sex with him was firmly stuck in her mind.

He had taken her to an upmarket restaurant that was frequented by showbiz celebrities.

There he wined and dined her, he was very pleasant and he managed to show her his charming side.

At the end of the evening when it was time to leave Powell suggested that they go back to his place to discuss her terms of employment.

Mellissa's reply to the proposal was. "I had better be getting home now as Joseph will be expecting me."

Powell's answer to that was. "Of course if you are not really that keen on the position. There are thousands of other young ladies like yourself that are."

When she arrived home a little after 5.30 a.m. Joseph was in bed fast asleep.

She undressed and took a shower, the tears were pouring down her face as the water from the shower head flowed down her naked body.

What she had done in order to secure the position of Powell's personal assistant and judge on his television show made her feel sick to the bottom of her stomach.

And so when Mellissa looked at Powell with that yes you did look, every person present knew that what Answell had said was the truth.

Powell bowed his head. For the first time in his life he felt vulnerable and exposed. This made him feel ashamed.

Answell continued. 'If you did not have sex with him you would have not got your job. You had to compromise yourself in order to get the job you so dearly wanted. That no good scumbag uses and abuses everyone he meets in order to get whatever it is he wants, he has trodden every person he meets into the ground, he has no conscience, but no more, we will ruin him.'

Mellissa now had tears streaming down her face as she said pleadingly. 'No you don't understand.'

'I do understand, I understand only too well.'

'No you don't, when I got the job, I called my mother to tell her, because I was so excited. My mother is still living in Kenya but she told me things about Trenton Powell. She explained to me that it's not his real name. I never knew that my mother had even heard of him until then. She then told me things about him that I never knew. I had moved back to England when I was eighteen. My mother stayed in Kenya.'

Answell was baffled and becoming agitated. 'What has that got to do with anything?' He yelled.

'When I was six years old my mother took me to Kenya. I remember how excited I was seeing the Lions and the Elephants, but we never went home, at first I didn't understand why, I really missed home and my friends, but most of all I missed my dad. For a long time I kept asking mum. "When are we going home?" She just said "This is our home now." For a long time I cried myself to sleep. And I started wetting the bed, which mother would scold me for. It was as I got older I realised the reason that we didn't go home was because mother was having a relationship with a barman that worked in the hotel that we were staying in. That was why we set up home there. When I got into my teens I started wondering why it was that we lived in a nice house whilst people all around us were living in poverty. Then one night when mother was drunk she explained that daddy would pay a large sum of money into her bank account each month so that I would be provided for, despite the fact that she would not allow him to see me or communicate with me in any way. Her exact words were. "He is a spineless git and I can wrap him around my little finger, he deserves to be taken for every penny that I can get from him." Because I was only a little girl at the time my memories are blurred, but I can remember him being the most loving caring daddy that any girl could wish for. He called me his Cherry Pie and he would sing to me. "Hush little baby don't you cry Daddy loves his Cherry Pie." Trenton Powell is my father.'

The Arrest

Ainsdale and Shanklin followed by four other plain
clothes police officers rushed onto the stage.

As one police officer was putting handcuffs on George
Answell, whilst forcing his arms behind his back.

Ainsdale was saying. 'George Answell I am arresting on
suspicion of the murder of Christopher Charles Farrington.
You don't need to say anything although it may harm your
defence if you fail to …..'

Jason cut in. 'It was not him. He hasn't killed anybody. It
was me, I killed that lowlife parasite.'

'What are you saying?' Asked Detective Inspector
Ainsdale.

'I am saying I killed Chris the Greek. That's what I am
saying. He threatened to expose us.'

Powell cut in. 'Shut up Jason. You are interfering with the
police in the course of their duty.'

'No Trenton Baby! I am not interfering with the police, I
am helping them with their enquiries. I killed the ponce.'

Shanklin looked at Jason and said. 'Are you trying to tell
us that it was you that killed Christopher Charles
Farrington?'

'I am not trying to tell you, I am telling you. In fact I have
said it three times already. I killed that no good piece of
shit that calls himself Chris the Greek.'

'Jason shut up.' Yelled Powell.

Jason carried on speaking. 'One evening after a hard days
filming, Trenton and I went to the Ivy club, we had drunk

an enormous amount of pink bubbly. When we were
approached by this big shot music promoter. He was quite
charming. He showed us some photographs of himself
with some of the biggest names in showbiz. He was name
dropping all over the place. He wanted to go into business
with Trenton. Well to cut a long story short, Trenton
invited him back to our place and we finished up having a
threesome.'

Powell lunged at Jason and putting his hands around his
throat he began to strangle him.

The police pulled Powell off and cuffed him.

When Jason had composed himself he carried on. 'The
next day Trenton ran a check on this man that called
himself "Chris the Greek." It turned out that he had never
worked in the music industry or any industry in his entire
life. He was a fraudster with two previous convictions.
Trenton said we were to have nothing to do with him. But
he kept calling and he threatened to go to the press and tell
them about the naughty night we had. He said the papers
would pay him £200,000 for a story like that, and all we
had to do was give him £100,000 and he would go away.
He said he would disappear to Thailand. Trenton was
fuming, it wasn't the money £100,000 is petty cash to him.
It was the thought that some no good lowlife had one over
on him. "I will kill the slimy scumbag." Was what Trenton
said. I told him to leave it to me and I would sort it. And
so I did, I made the parasite disappear. And what thanks
do I get? Shit. That's what I get shit for thanks. Well no
more, it's over between us Trenton Baby.'

And They All Lived Happily Ever After

Jason pleaded guilty to the Murder of Christopher Charles
Farrington and was sentenced to seven years in prison.

Powell got convicted of assaulting Jason and was given
200 hours community service, which he refused to do **as**
he felt that it was beneath him. For going against the
wishes of the court he spent ninety days in prison.
Following his release he went into hiding and was never
seen in the public eye ever again.

George Answell never got over the grief of losing his
beloved daughter. He turned to alcohol for comfort and
very soon was drinking two bottles of whisky per day.
He died two years later from liver failure.

Mellissa and Mary-Anne decided that men were not for
them, they got married and settled down together, but their
relationship lasted barely a year, as Mellissa could not get
over losing Joseph. It was when she called his name
during the moment of passion that Mary-Anne decided
enough is enough.

Amellia and her parents went back to being a loving family. They sold their house and moved into a council flat to pay for Amellia to go to the best clinic available for drug rehabilitation.

When she was in the clinic her parents visited her every day, they laughed and joked and made plans for Amellia's future. They were constantly talking about the exciting times they would have when she came out of rehab.

Six months passed and Amellia was completely clean, there was no danger of her ever going back to her drug taking lifestyle.

On the morning that Amellia was being released her parents were so excited, they decorated the flat with tin foil helium filled balloons.

When they got to the clinic to pick Amellia up, she was already standing outside the main front entrance.

As they parked their vehicle in the car park across the road from the clinic. The extremely excited Amellia called out to them. "Mummy, Daddy I am cured. I love you."

She then ran to join them, to jump into their loving arms. Tragically due to the immense excitement she forgot to look for traffic and was hit by a bus.

Only in fairy stories, do the main characters live.

"Happily Ever After."

Conscience

Three strangers with nothing in common find themselves trapped together in a hell of their own making.

A bitter twisted middle aged woman.

A compassionate teenager with a cross to bear.

And a misogynistic police officer.

As the story unfolds we see that they are not so different.

Conscience is a fictional tale based on actual events.

Where does the fiction end and the truth begin?

Described as an "Emotional rollercoaster" Conscience has the audience laughing out loud. Then it takes them where most author' fear to tread.

False evidence that got an innocent teenage boy hung.

Infidelity that destroys a marriage.

Physical abuse at the hands of a mother's lover.

Are just a few issues that Conscience dares to broach.

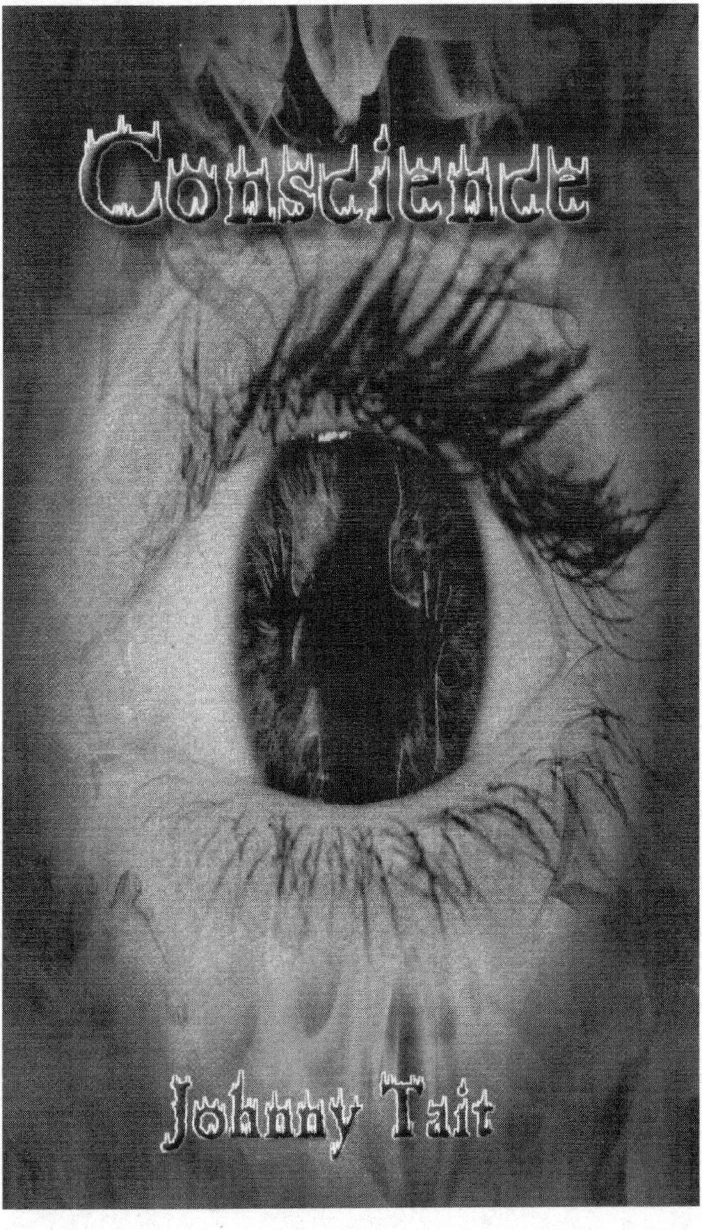
Conscience
Johnny Tait